KEAN SOO

MARCH GRAND PRIX

THE GREAT DESERT RALLY

STONE ARCH BOOKS
a capstone imprint

March Grand Prix
published by Stone Arch Books,
a Capstone Imprint
1710 Roe Crest Drive
North Mankato, Minnesota 56003
www.capstonepub.com

Cataloging-in-Publication Data is available on
the Library of Congress website.

ISBN: 978-1-4342-9641-2 (library hardcover)
ISBN: 978-1-4342-9644-3 (paperback)
ISBN: 978-1-4965-0186-8 (eBook)

Summary: A new, turbo-charged graphic novel
by Kean Soo, author of the acclaimed, award-
winning series Jellaby. March Hare wants to be
the fastest and furriest race car driver around.
But first, this rabbit racer will have to prove his
skill at the speedway, on the streets, and in the
desert. With pedal-to-the-metal illustrations and
full-throttle action, March is sure to be a winner!

Printed in China by Nordica.
0415/CA21500596
042015   008843NORDF15

To Tory,

For being the best co-driver I could ever ask for.

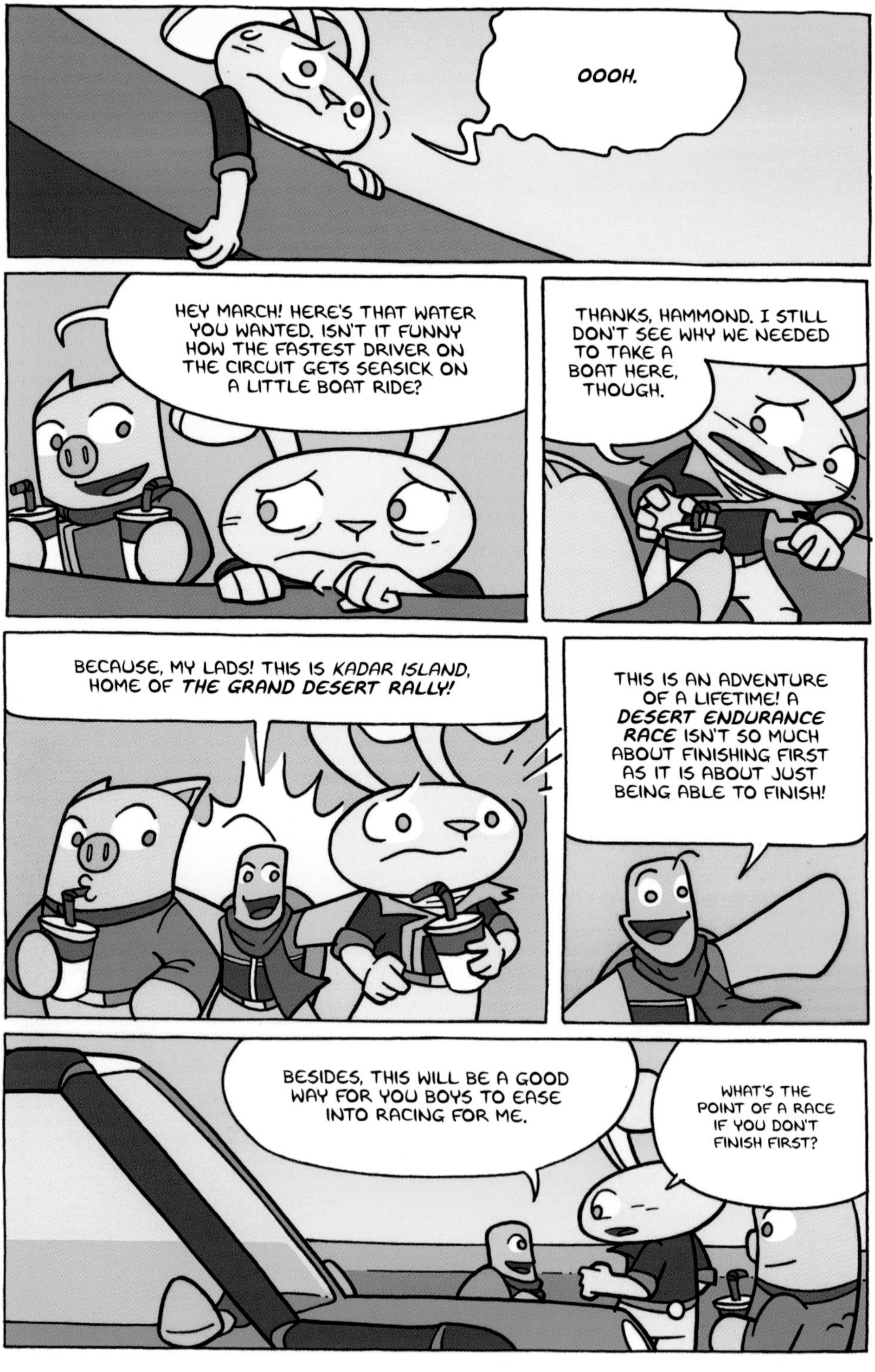
OOOH.
HEY MARCH! HERE'S THAT WATER YOU WANTED. ISN'T IT FUNNY HOW THE FASTEST DRIVER ON THE CIRCUIT GETS SEASICK ON A LITTLE BOAT RIDE?
THANKS, HAMMOND. I STILL DON'T SEE WHY WE NEEDED TO TAKE A BOAT HERE, THOUGH.
BECAUSE, MY LADS! THIS IS KADAR ISLAND, HOME OF THE GRAND DESERT RALLY!
THIS IS AN ADVENTURE OF A LIFETIME! A DESERT ENDURANCE RACE ISN'T SO MUCH ABOUT FINISHING FIRST AS IT IS ABOUT JUST BEING ABLE TO FINISH!
BESIDES, THIS WILL BE A GOOD WAY FOR YOU BOYS TO EASE INTO RACING FOR ME.
WHAT'S THE POINT OF A RACE IF YOU DON'T FINISH FIRST?

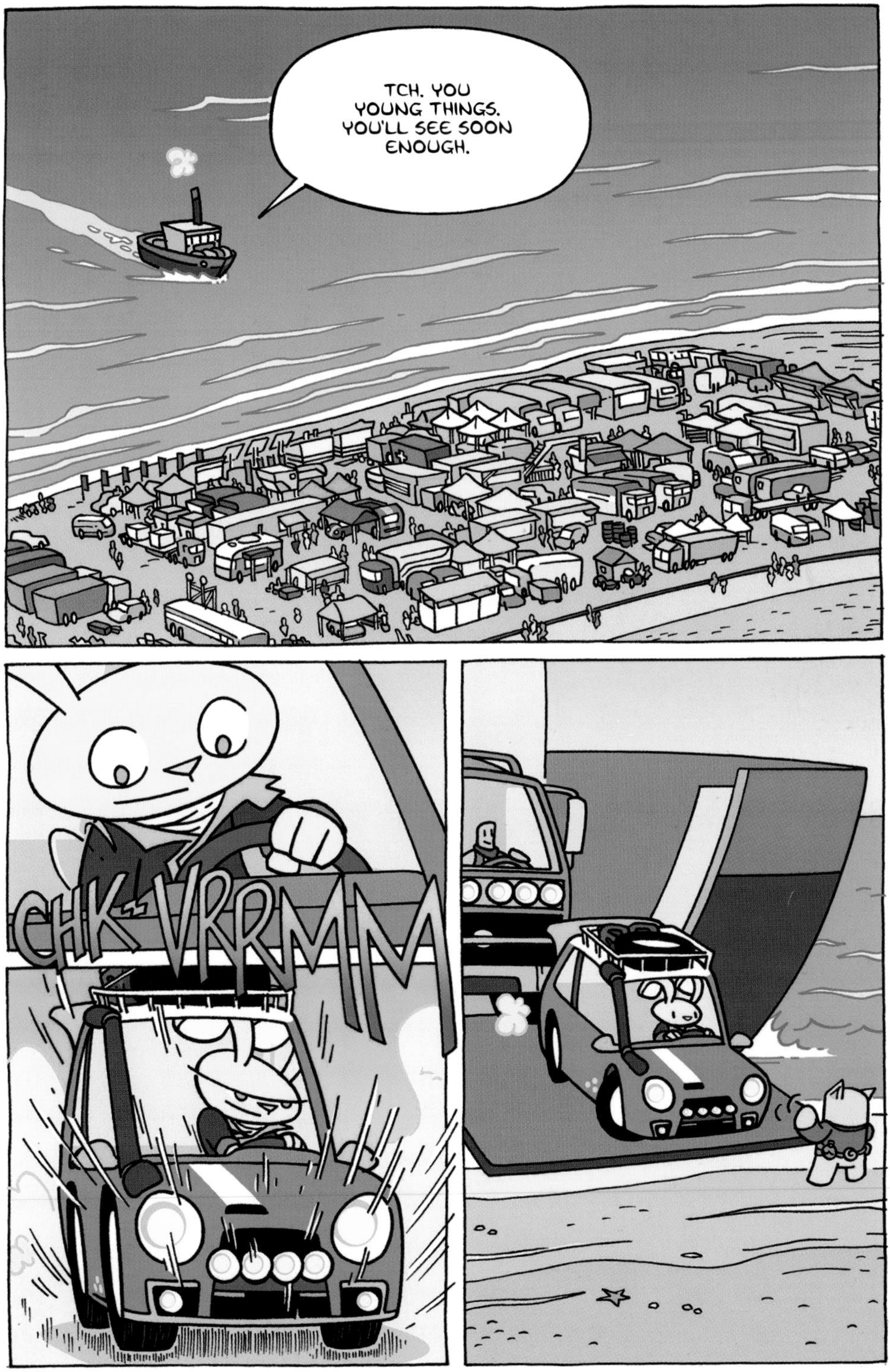
TCH. YOU YOUNG THINGS. YOU'LL SEE SOON ENOUGH.
CHK-VRRMM

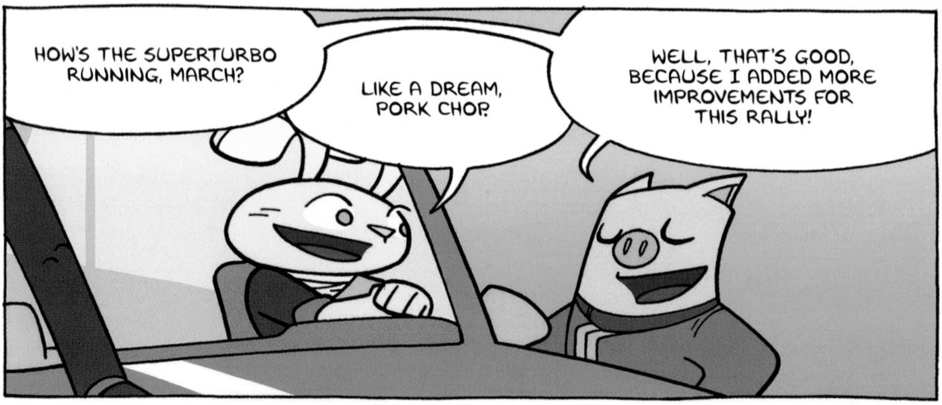
HOW'S THE SUPERTURBO RUNNING, MARCH?
LIKE A DREAM, PORK CHOP.
WELL, THAT'S GOOD, BECAUSE I ADDED MORE IMPROVEMENTS FOR THIS RALLY!

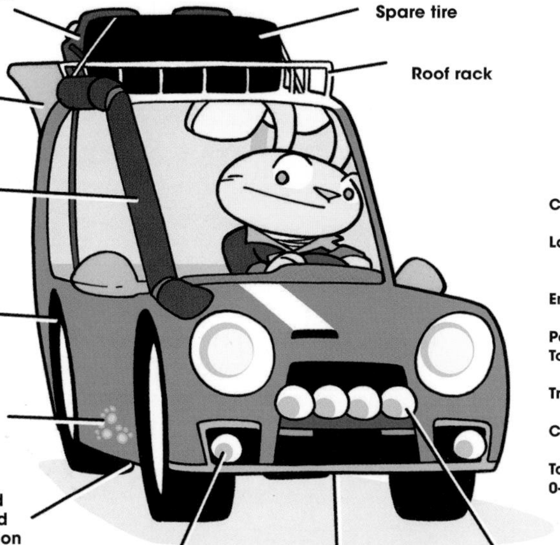
Spare gasoline canisters
Spare tire
Extra large spoiler
Roof rack
Engine snorkel
Reinforced rally tires
June Hare's lucky paw prints
Raised off-road suspension
High-intensity fog lamps
Reinforced underside skid plate
Auxilliary driving lamps

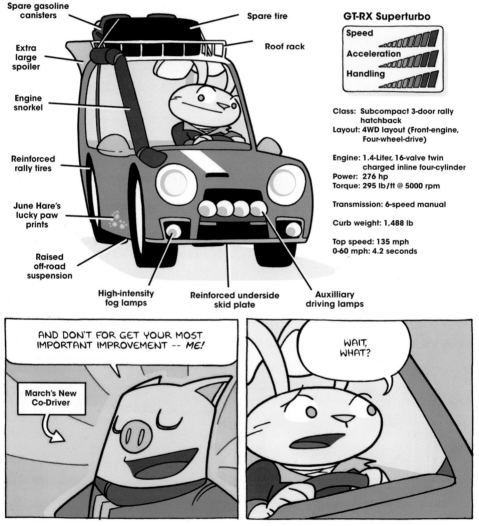

GT-RX Superturbo

Speed

Acceleration

Handling

Class: Subcompact 3-door rally hatchback
Layout: 4WD layout (Front-engine, Four-wheel-drive)

Engine: 1.4-Liter, 16-valve twin charged inline four-cylinder
Power: 276 hp
Torque: 295 lb/ft @ 5000 rpm

Transmission: 6-speed manual

Curb weight: 1,488 lb

Top speed: 135 mph
0-60 mph: 4.2 seconds

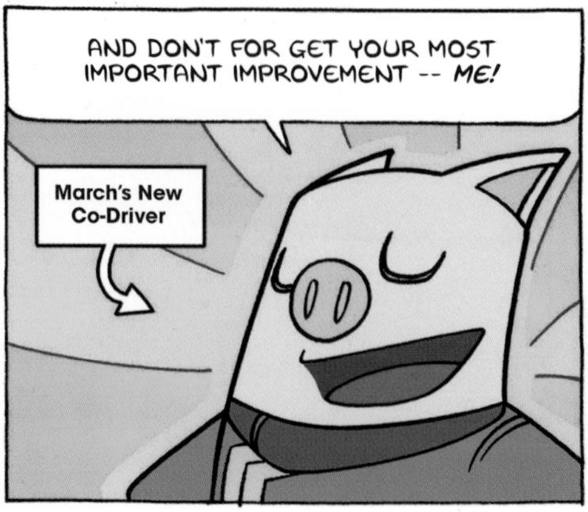
AND DON'T FOR GET YOUR MOST IMPORTANT IMPROVEMENT -- ME!
March's New Co-Driver

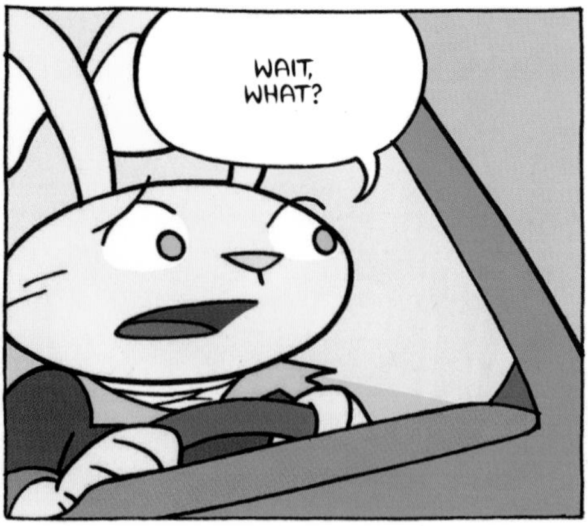
WAIT, WHAT?

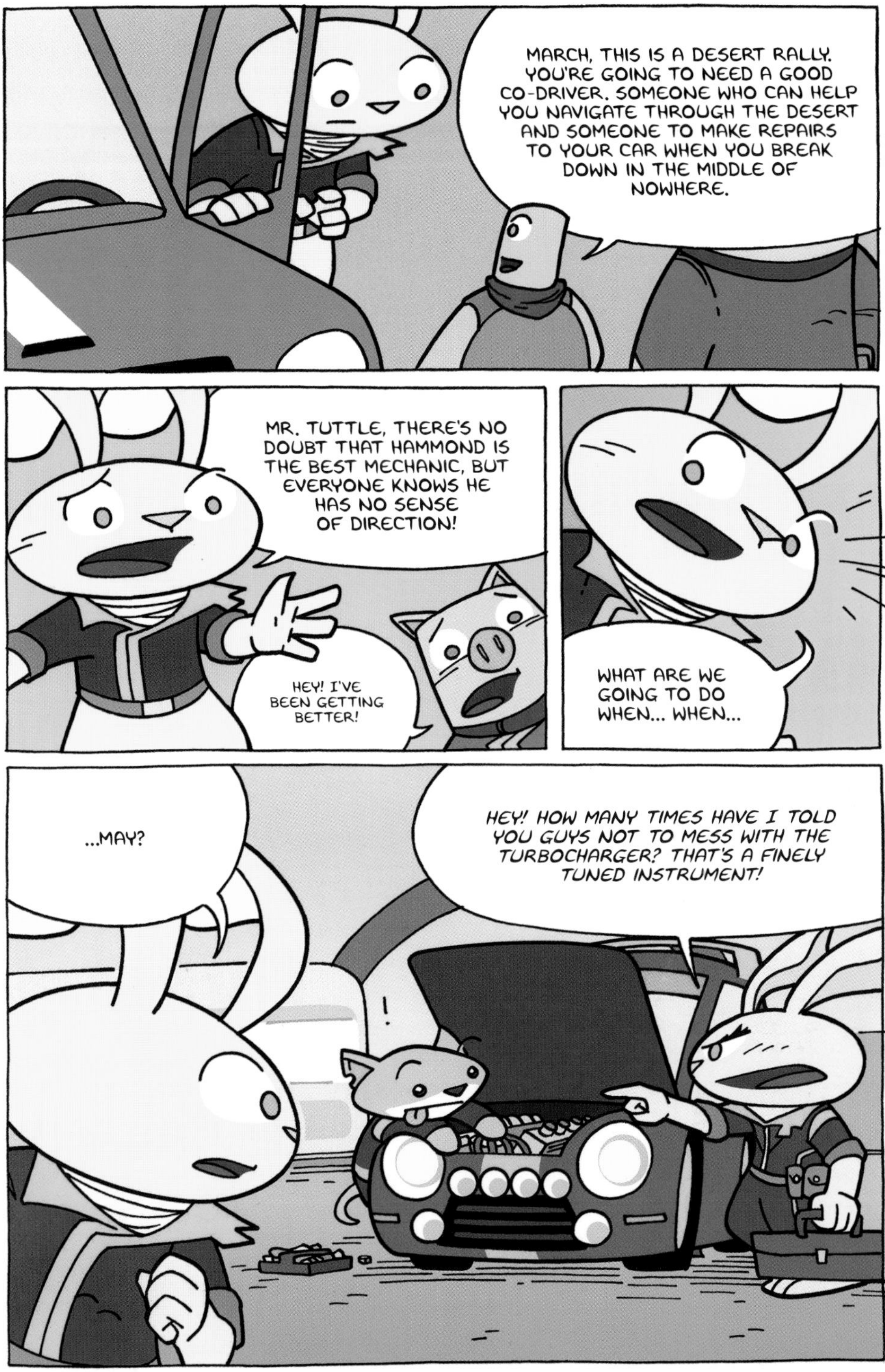
MARCH, THIS IS A DESERT RALLY. YOU'RE GOING TO NEED A GOOD CO-DRIVER. SOMEONE WHO CAN HELP YOU NAVIGATE THROUGH THE DESERT AND SOMEONE TO MAKE REPAIRS TO YOUR CAR WHEN YOU BREAK DOWN IN THE MIDDLE OF NOWHERE.
MR. TUTTLE, THERE'S NO DOUBT THAT HAMMOND IS THE BEST MECHANIC, BUT EVERYONE KNOWS HE HAS NO SENSE OF DIRECTION!
HEY! I'VE BEEN GETTING BETTER!
WHAT ARE WE GOING TO DO WHEN... WHEN...
...MAY?
HEY! HOW MANY TIMES HAVE I TOLD YOU GUYS NOT TO MESS WITH THE TURBOCHARGER? THAT'S A FINELY TUNED INSTRUMENT!
!

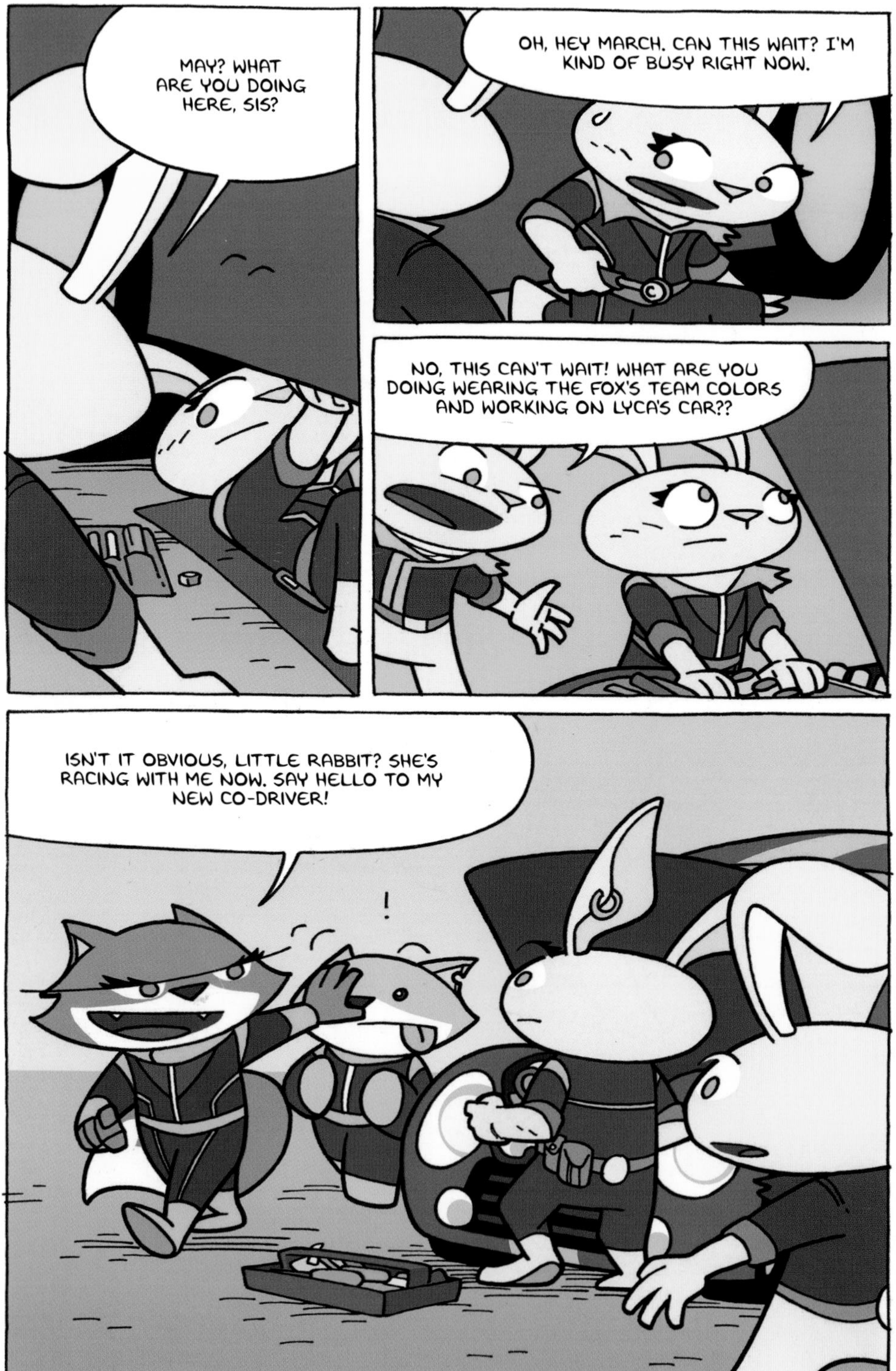
MAY? WHAT ARE YOU DOING HERE, SIS?
OH, HEY MARCH. CAN THIS WAIT? I'M KIND OF BUSY RIGHT NOW.
NO, THIS CAN'T WAIT! WHAT ARE YOU DOING WEARING THE FOX'S TEAM COLORS AND WORKING ON LYCA'S CAR??
ISN'T IT OBVIOUS, LITTLE RABBIT? SHE'S RACING WITH ME NOW. SAY HELLO TO MY NEW CO-DRIVER!
!

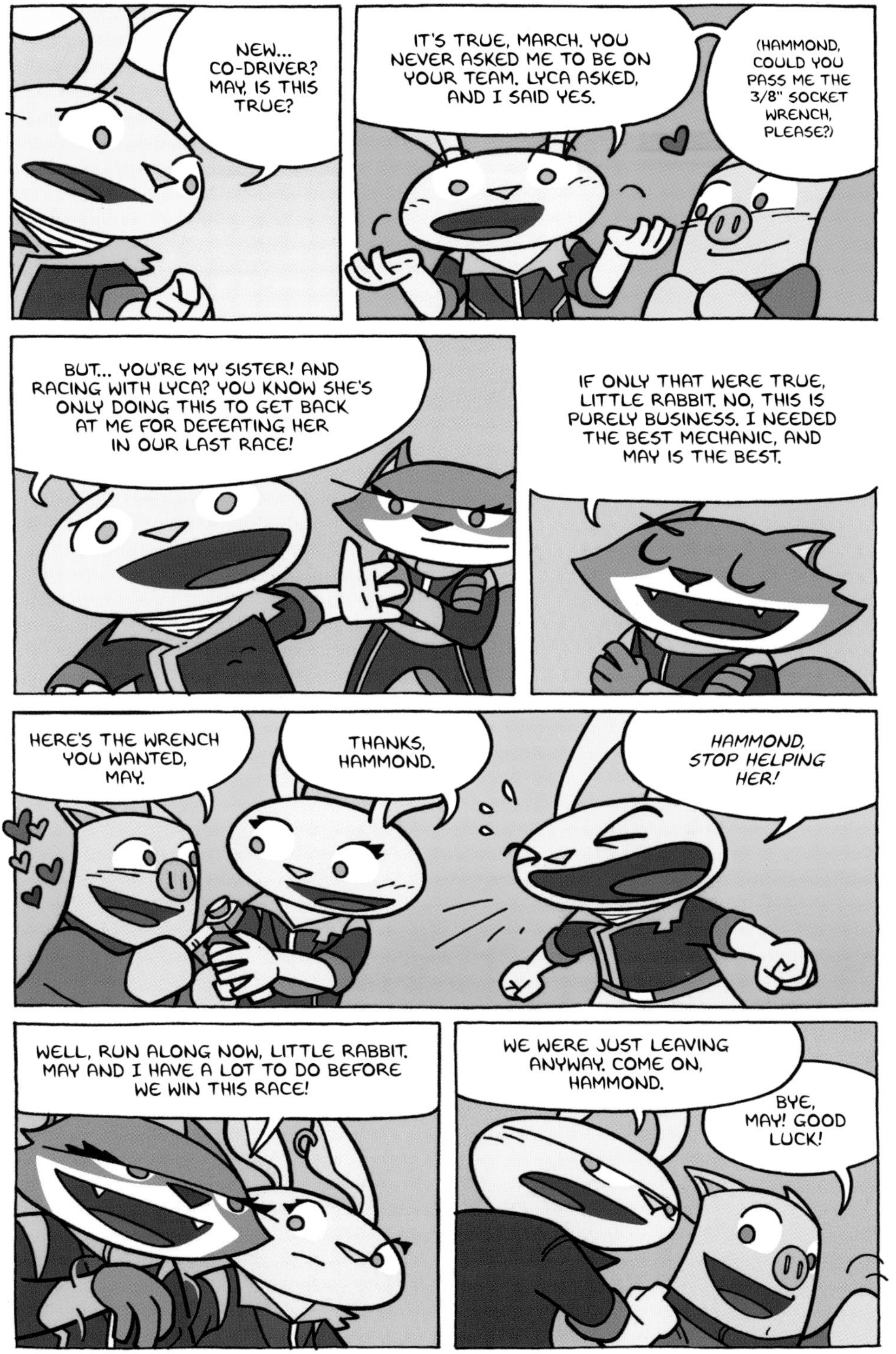
NEW... CO-DRIVER? MAY, IS THIS TRUE?
IT'S TRUE, MARCH. YOU NEVER ASKED ME TO BE ON YOUR TEAM. LYCA ASKED, AND I SAID YES.
(HAMMOND, COULD YOU PASS ME THE 3/8" SOCKET WRENCH, PLEASE?)
BUT... YOU'RE MY SISTER! AND RACING WITH LYCA? YOU KNOW SHE'S ONLY DOING THIS TO GET BACK AT ME FOR DEFEATING HER IN OUR LAST RACE!
IF ONLY THAT WERE TRUE, LITTLE RABBIT. NO, THIS IS PURELY BUSINESS. I NEEDED THE BEST MECHANIC, AND MAY IS THE BEST.
HERE'S THE WRENCH YOU WANTED, MAY.
THANKS, HAMMOND.
HAMMOND, STOP HELPING HER!
WELL, RUN ALONG NOW, LITTLE RABBIT. MAY AND I HAVE A LOT TO DO BEFORE WE WIN THIS RACE!
WE WERE JUST LEAVING ANYWAY. COME ON, HAMMOND.
BYE, MAY! GOOD LUCK!

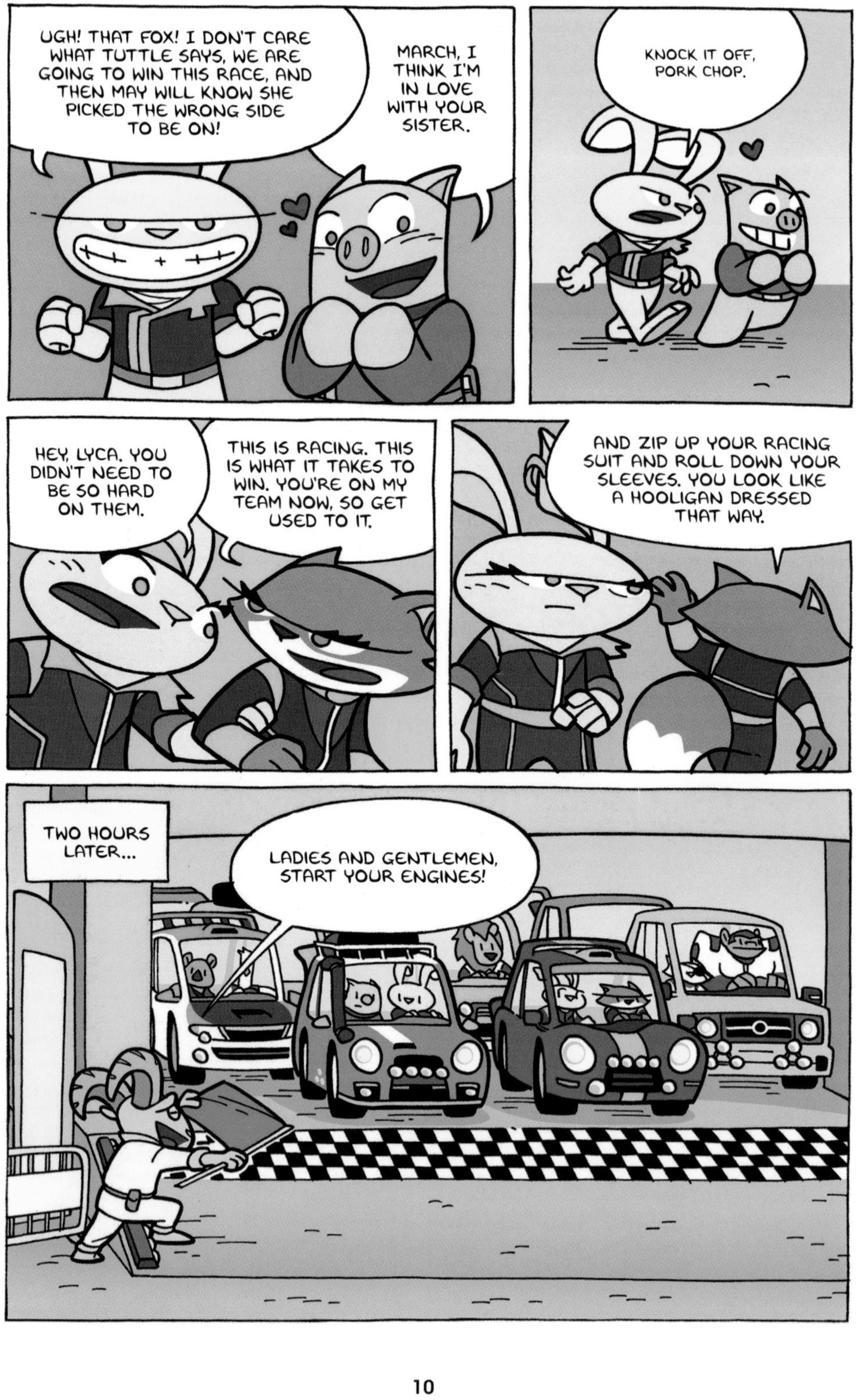
UGH! THAT FOX! I DON'T CARE WHAT TUTTLE SAYS, WE ARE GOING TO WIN THIS RACE, AND THEN MAY WILL KNOW SHE PICKED THE WRONG SIDE TO BE ON!
MARCH, I THINK I'M IN LOVE WITH YOUR SISTER.
KNOCK IT OFF, PORK CHOP.
HEY, LYCA. YOU DIDN'T NEED TO BE SO HARD ON THEM.
THIS IS RACING. THIS IS WHAT IT TAKES TO WIN. YOU'RE ON MY TEAM NOW, SO GET USED TO IT.
AND ZIP UP YOUR RACING SUIT AND ROLL DOWN YOUR SLEEVES. YOU LOOK LIKE A HOOLIGAN DRESSED THAT WAY.
TWO HOURS LATER...
LADIES AND GENTLEMEN, START YOUR ENGINES!

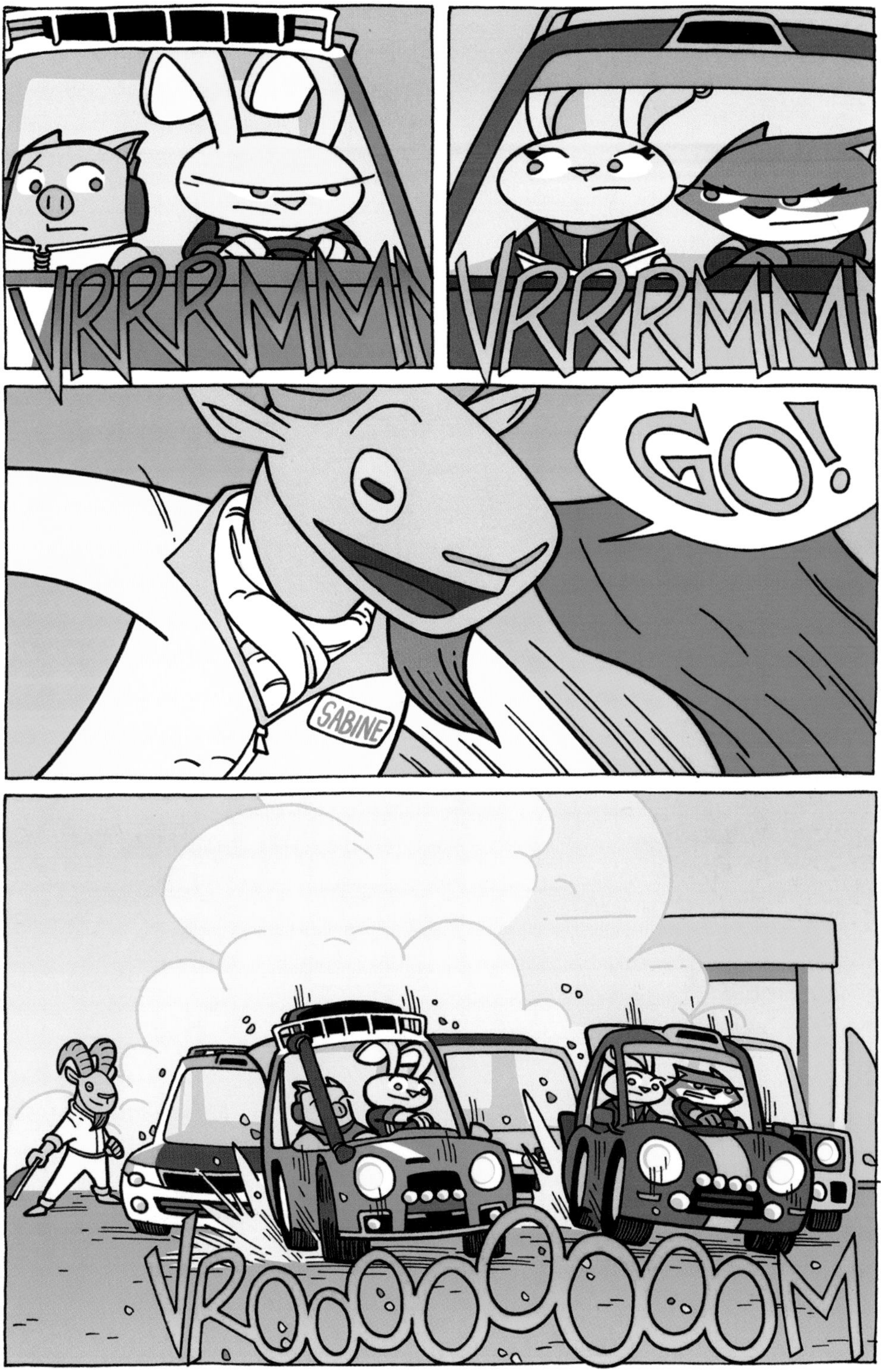
VRRRMMM
VRRRMMM
GO!
SABINE
VROOOOOOOOOM

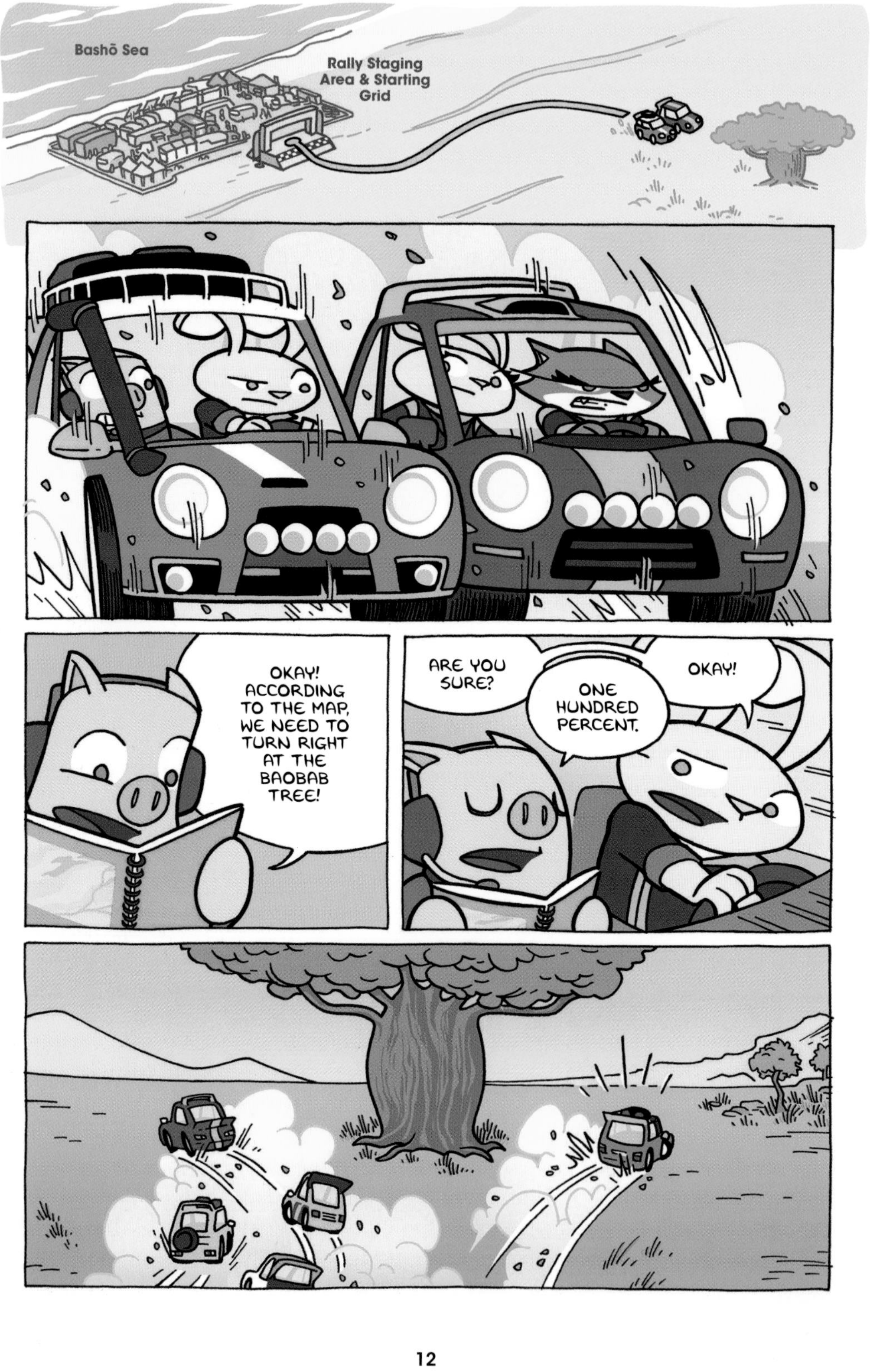
Bashō Sea
Rally Staging Area & Starting Grid
OKAY! ACCORDING TO THE MAP, WE NEED TO TURN RIGHT AT THE BAOBAB TREE!
ARE YOU SURE?
ONE HUNDRED PERCENT.
OKAY!

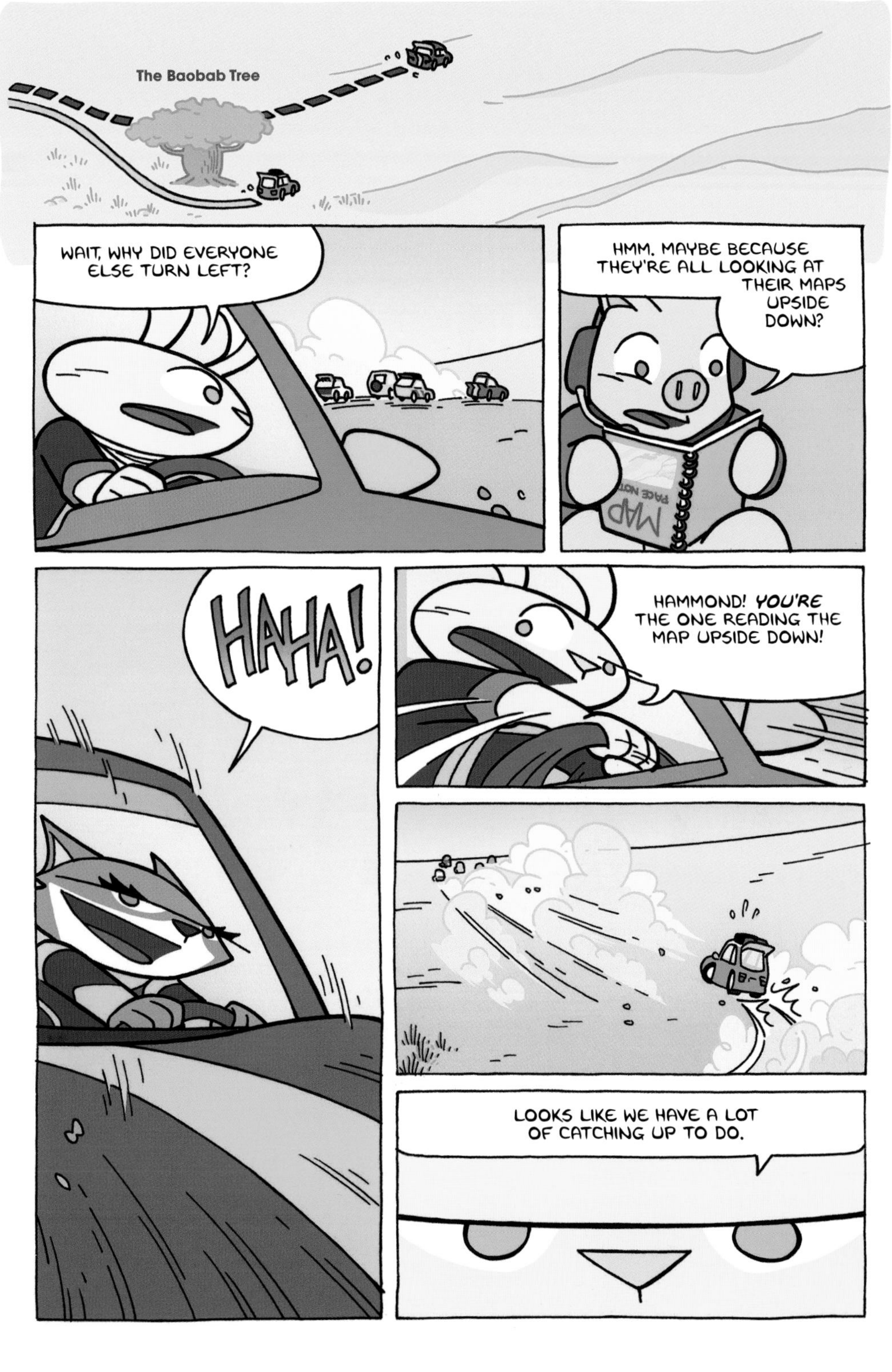
The Baobab Tree
WAIT, WHY DID EVERYONE ELSE TURN LEFT?
HMM. MAYBE BECAUSE THEY'RE ALL LOOKING AT THEIR MAPS UPSIDE DOWN?
MAP
HAHA!
HAMMOND! *YOU'RE* THE ONE READING THE MAP UPSIDE DOWN!
LOOKS LIKE WE HAVE A LOT OF CATCHING UP TO DO.

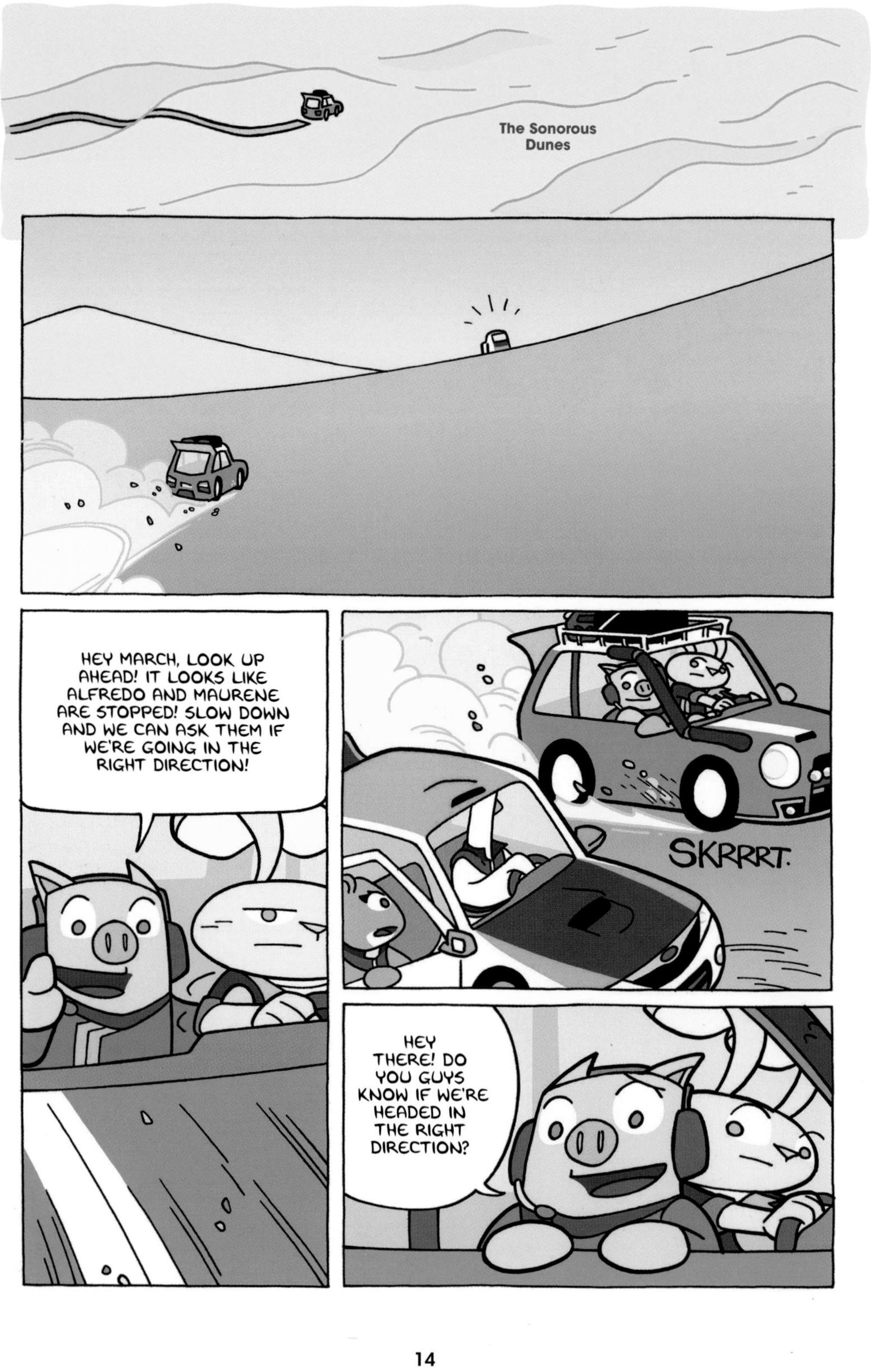
The Sonorous Dunes
HEY MARCH, LOOK UP AHEAD! IT LOOKS LIKE ALFREDO AND MAURENE ARE STOPPED! SLOW DOWN AND WE CAN ASK THEM IF WE'RE GOING IN THE RIGHT DIRECTION!
SKRRRT.
HEY THERE! DO YOU GUYS KNOW IF WE'RE HEADED IN THE RIGHT DIRECTION?

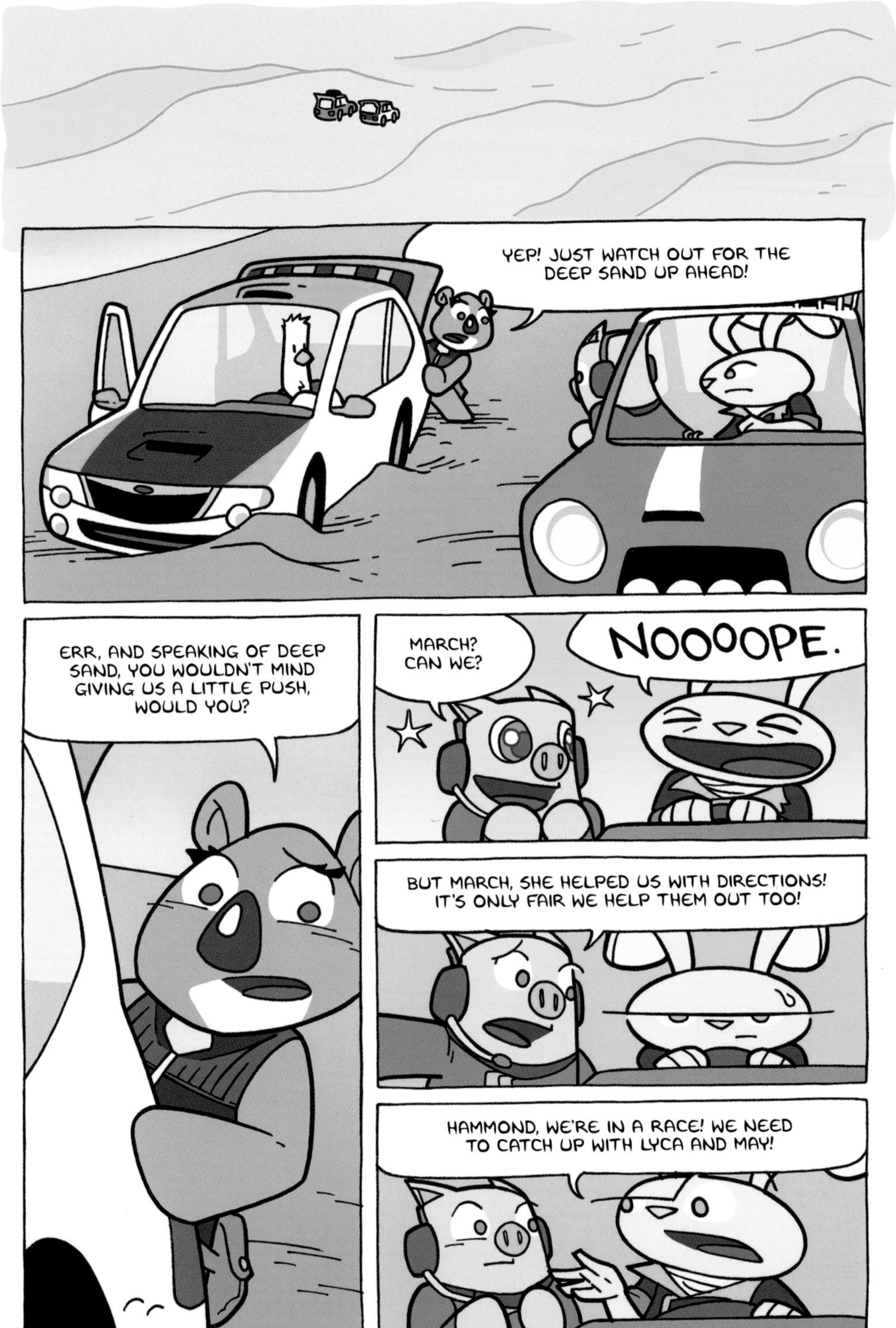
YEP! JUST WATCH OUT FOR THE DEEP SAND UP AHEAD!
ERR, AND SPEAKING OF DEEP SAND, YOU WOULDN'T MIND GIVING US A LITTLE PUSH, WOULD YOU?
MARCH? CAN WE?
NOOOOPE.
BUT MARCH, SHE HELPED US WITH DIRECTIONS! IT'S ONLY FAIR WE HELP THEM OUT TOO!
HAMMOND, WE'RE IN A RACE! WE NEED TO CATCH UP WITH LYCA AND MAY!

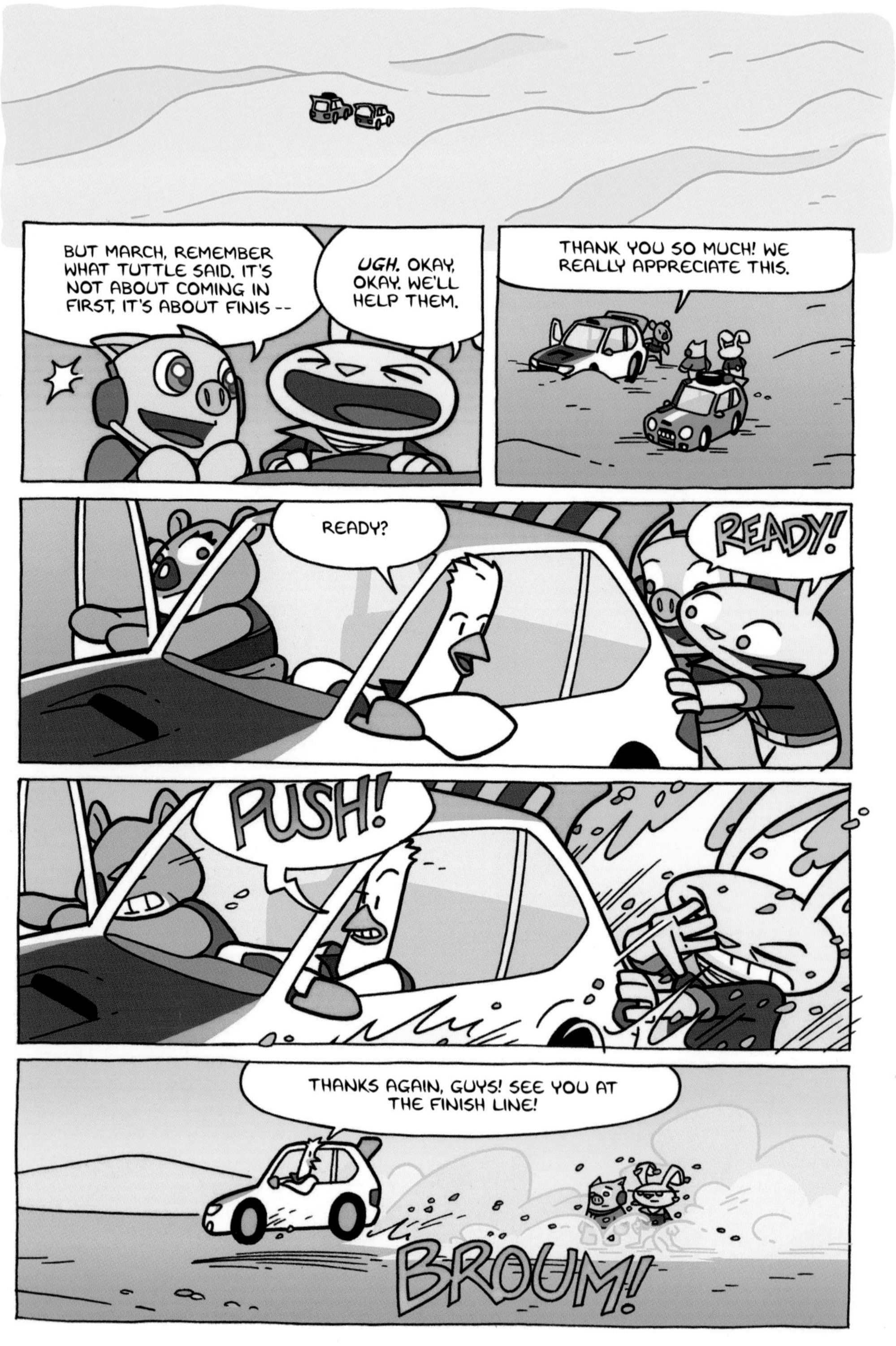
BUT MARCH, REMEMBER WHAT TUTTLE SAID. IT'S NOT ABOUT COMING IN FIRST, IT'S ABOUT FINIS --
UGH. OKAY, OKAY. WE'LL HELP THEM.
THANK YOU SO MUCH! WE REALLY APPRECIATE THIS.
READY?
READY!
PUSH!
THANKS AGAIN, GUYS! SEE YOU AT THE FINISH LINE!
BROUM!

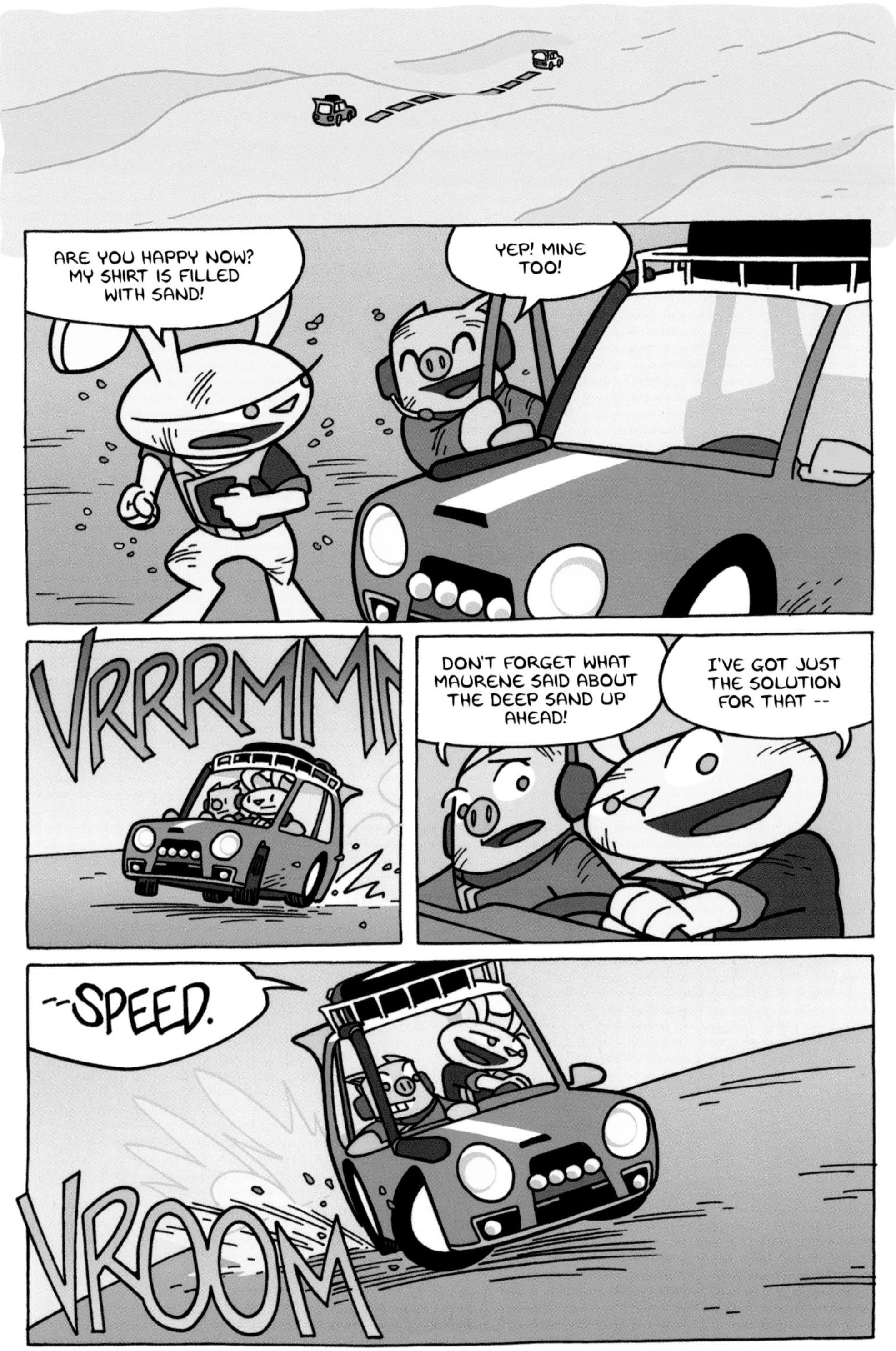
ARE YOU HAPPY NOW? MY SHIRT IS FILLED WITH SAND!
YEP! MINE TOO!
VRRRMMM
DON'T FORGET WHAT MAURENE SAID ABOUT THE DEEP SAND UP AHEAD!
I'VE GOT JUST THE SOLUTION FOR THAT --
--SPEED.
VROOM

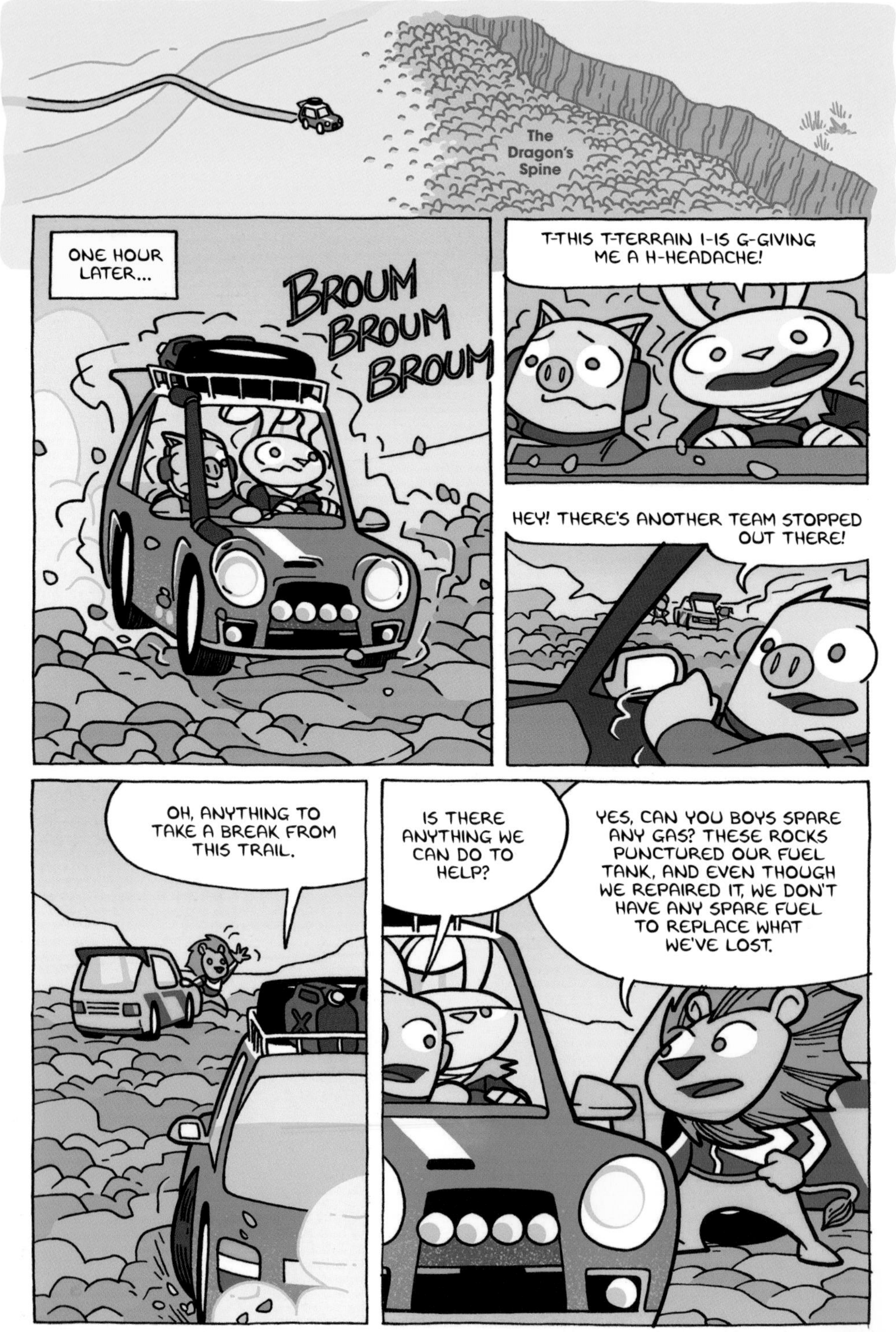
The Dragon's Spine
ONE HOUR LATER...
BROUM BROUM BROUM
T-THIS T-TERRAIN I-IS G-GIVING ME A H-HEADACHE!
HEY! THERE'S ANOTHER TEAM STOPPED OUT THERE!
OH, ANYTHING TO TAKE A BREAK FROM THIS TRAIL.
IS THERE ANYTHING WE CAN DO TO HELP?
YES, CAN YOU BOYS SPARE ANY GAS? THESE ROCKS PUNCTURED OUR FUEL TANK, AND EVEN THOUGH WE REPAIRED IT, WE DON'T HAVE ANY SPARE FUEL TO REPLACE WHAT WE'VE LOST.

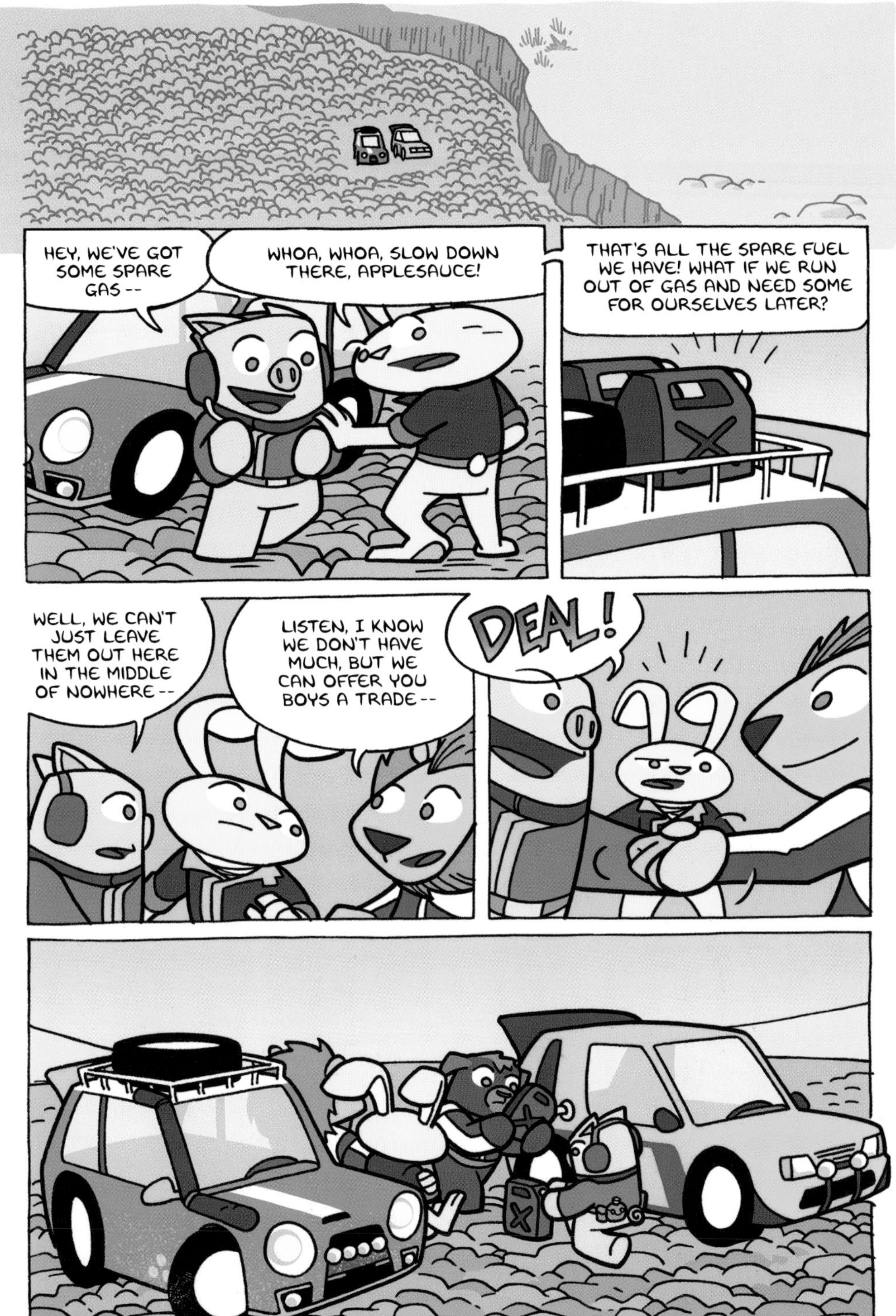
HEY, WE'VE GOT SOME SPARE GAS --
WHOA, WHOA, SLOW DOWN THERE, APPLESAUCE!
THAT'S ALL THE SPARE FUEL WE HAVE! WHAT IF WE RUN OUT OF GAS AND NEED SOME FOR OURSELVES LATER?
WELL, WE CAN'T JUST LEAVE THEM OUT HERE IN THE MIDDLE OF NOWHERE --
LISTEN, I KNOW WE DON'T HAVE MUCH, BUT WE CAN OFFER YOU BOYS A TRADE --
DEAL!

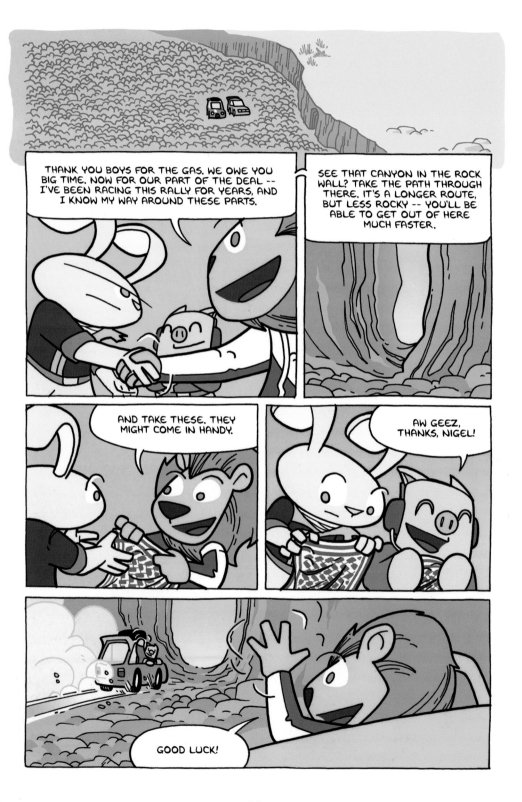

THANK YOU BOYS FOR THE GAS. WE OWE YOU BIG TIME. NOW FOR OUR PART OF THE DEAL -- I'VE BEEN RACING THIS RALLY FOR YEARS, AND I KNOW MY WAY AROUND THESE PARTS.

SEE THAT CANYON IN THE ROCK WALL? TAKE THE PATH THROUGH THERE. IT'S A LONGER ROUTE, BUT LESS ROCKY -- YOU'LL BE ABLE TO GET OUT OF HERE MUCH FASTER.

AND TAKE THESE. THEY MIGHT COME IN HANDY.

AW GEEZ, THANKS, NIGEL!

GOOD LUCK!

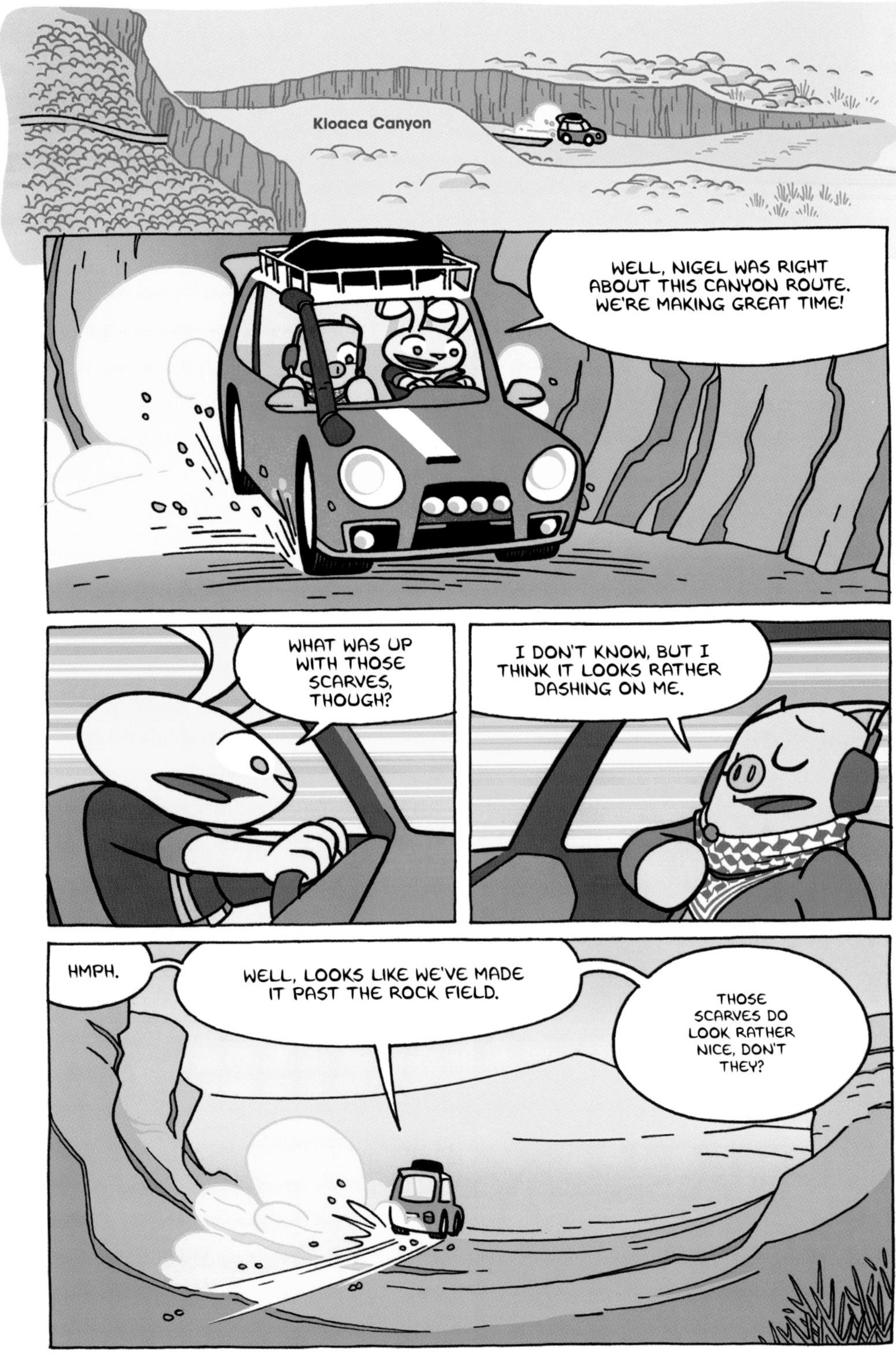
Kloaca Canyon
WELL, NIGEL WAS RIGHT ABOUT THIS CANYON ROUTE. WE'RE MAKING GREAT TIME!
WHAT WAS UP WITH THOSE SCARVES, THOUGH?
I DON'T KNOW, BUT I THINK IT LOOKS RATHER DASHING ON ME.
HMPH.
WELL, LOOKS LIKE WE'VE MADE IT PAST THE ROCK FIELD.
THOSE SCARVES DO LOOK RATHER NICE, DON'T THEY?

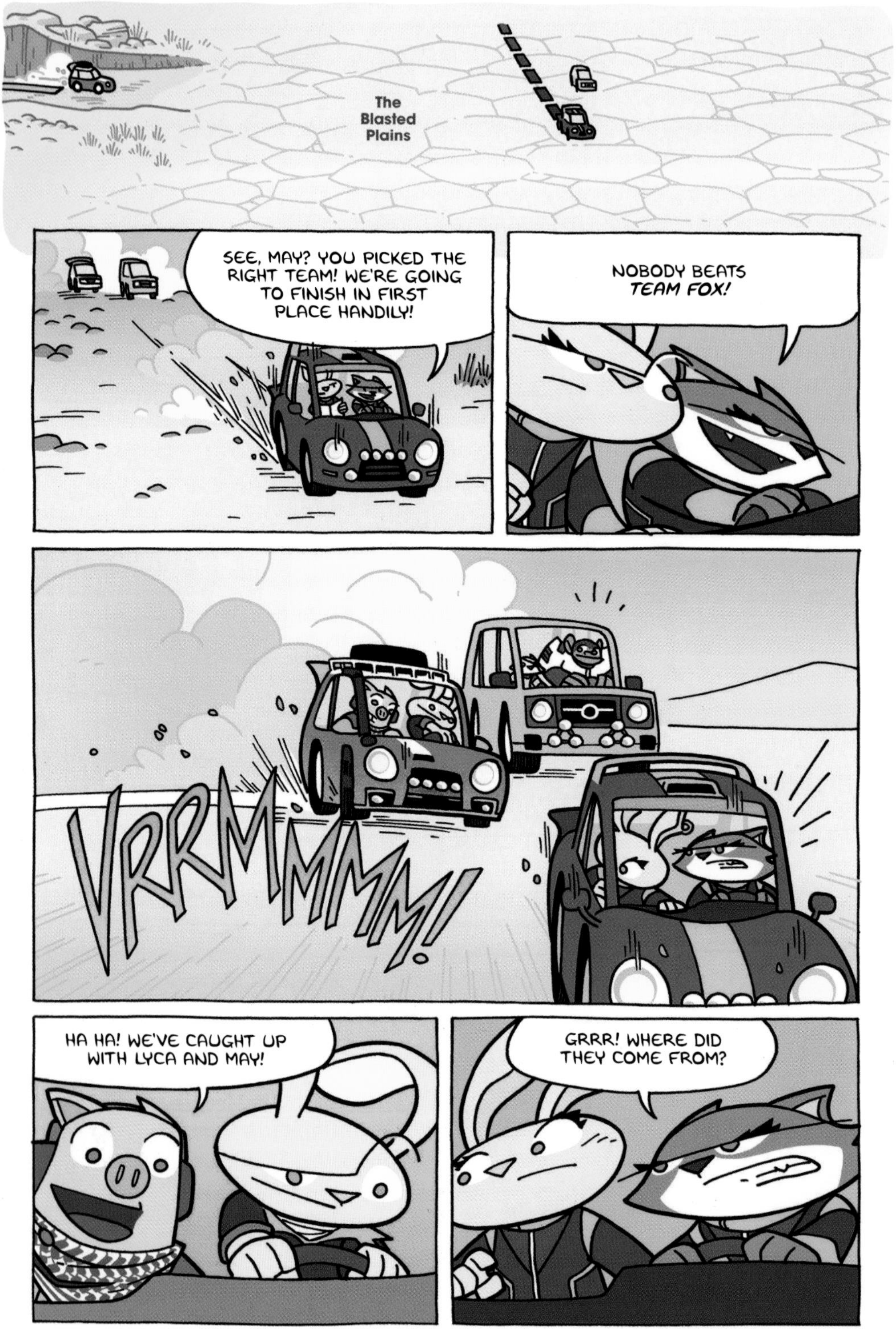
The Blasted Plains
SEE, MAY? YOU PICKED THE RIGHT TEAM! WE'RE GOING TO FINISH IN FIRST PLACE HANDILY!
NOBODY BEATS *TEAM FOX!*
VRRMMMM!
HA HA! WE'VE CAUGHT UP WITH LYCA AND MAY!
GRRR! WHERE DID THEY COME FROM?

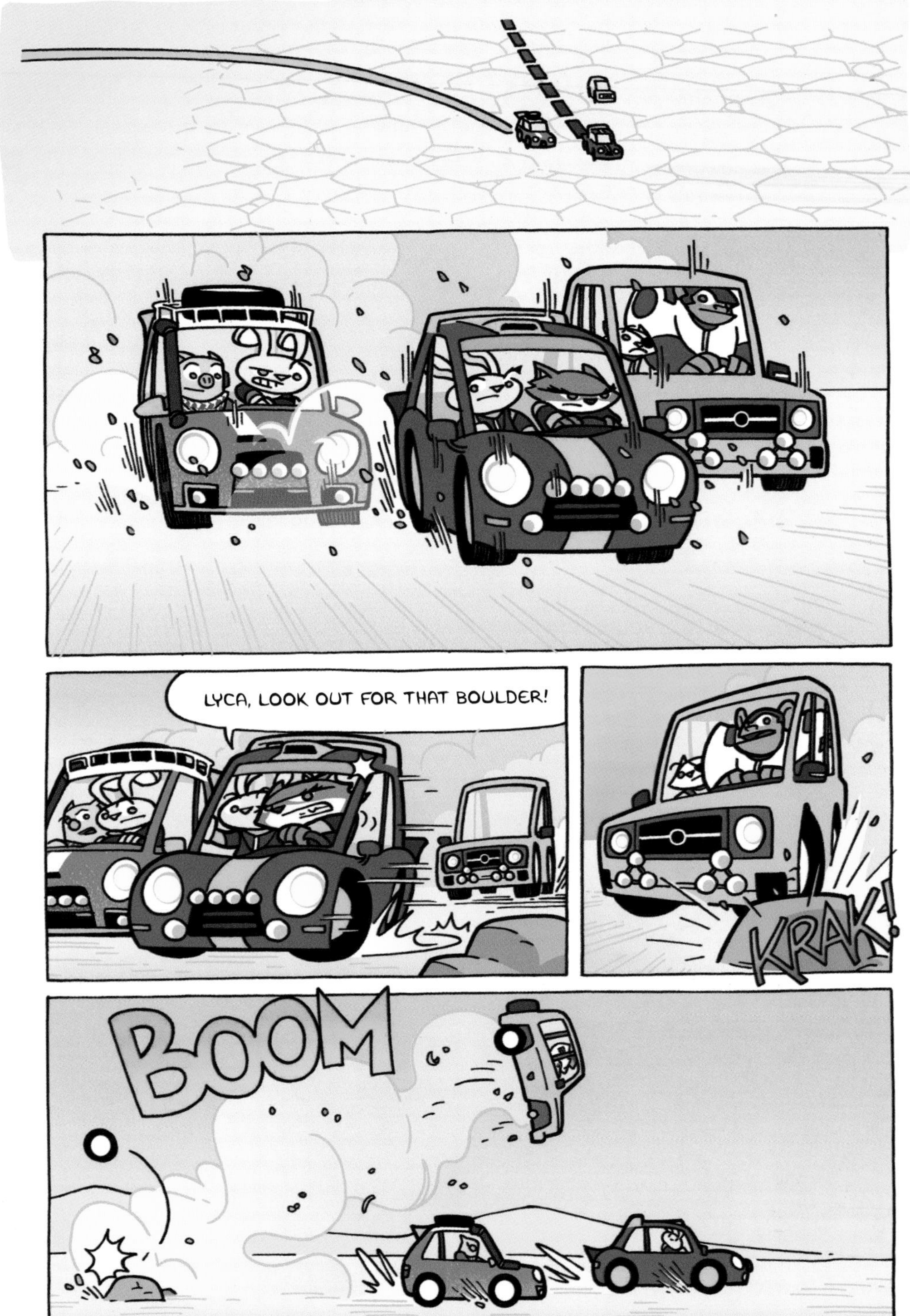
LYCA, LOOK OUT FOR THAT BOULDER!
KRAK!
BOOM

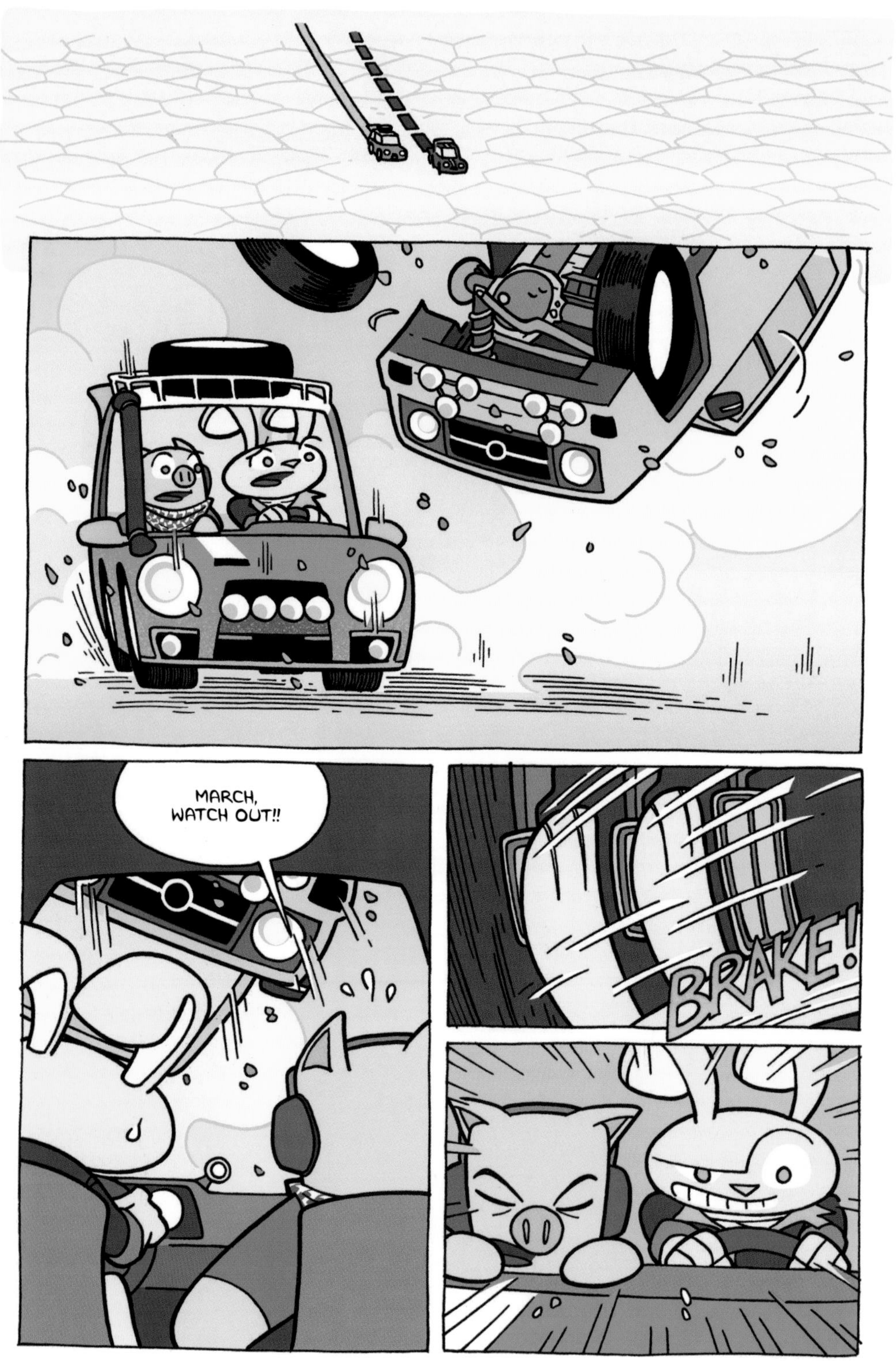
MARCH,
WATCH OUT!!
BRAKE!

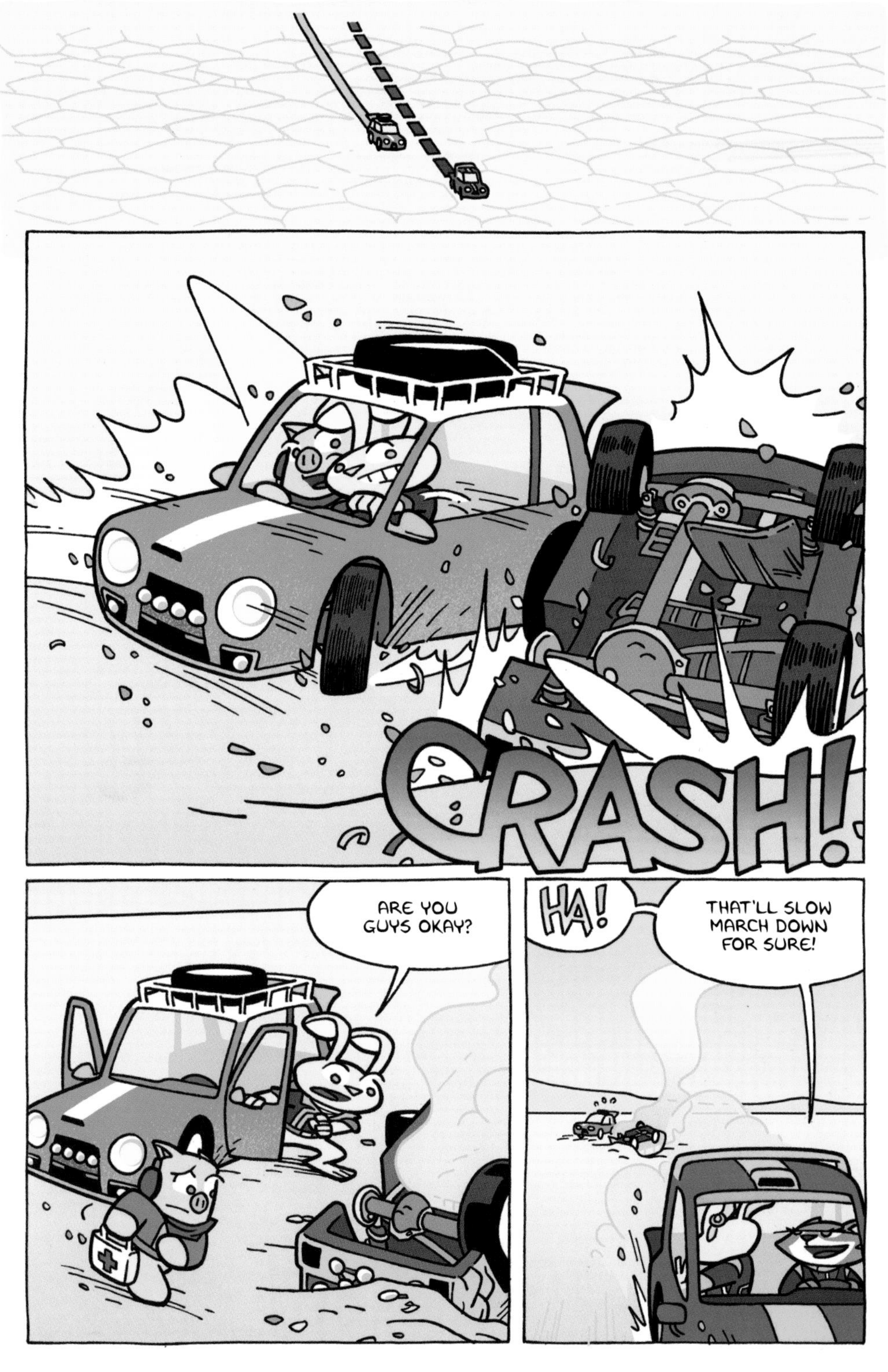
CRASH!
ARE YOU GUYS OKAY?
HA!
THAT'LL SLOW MARCH DOWN FOR SURE!

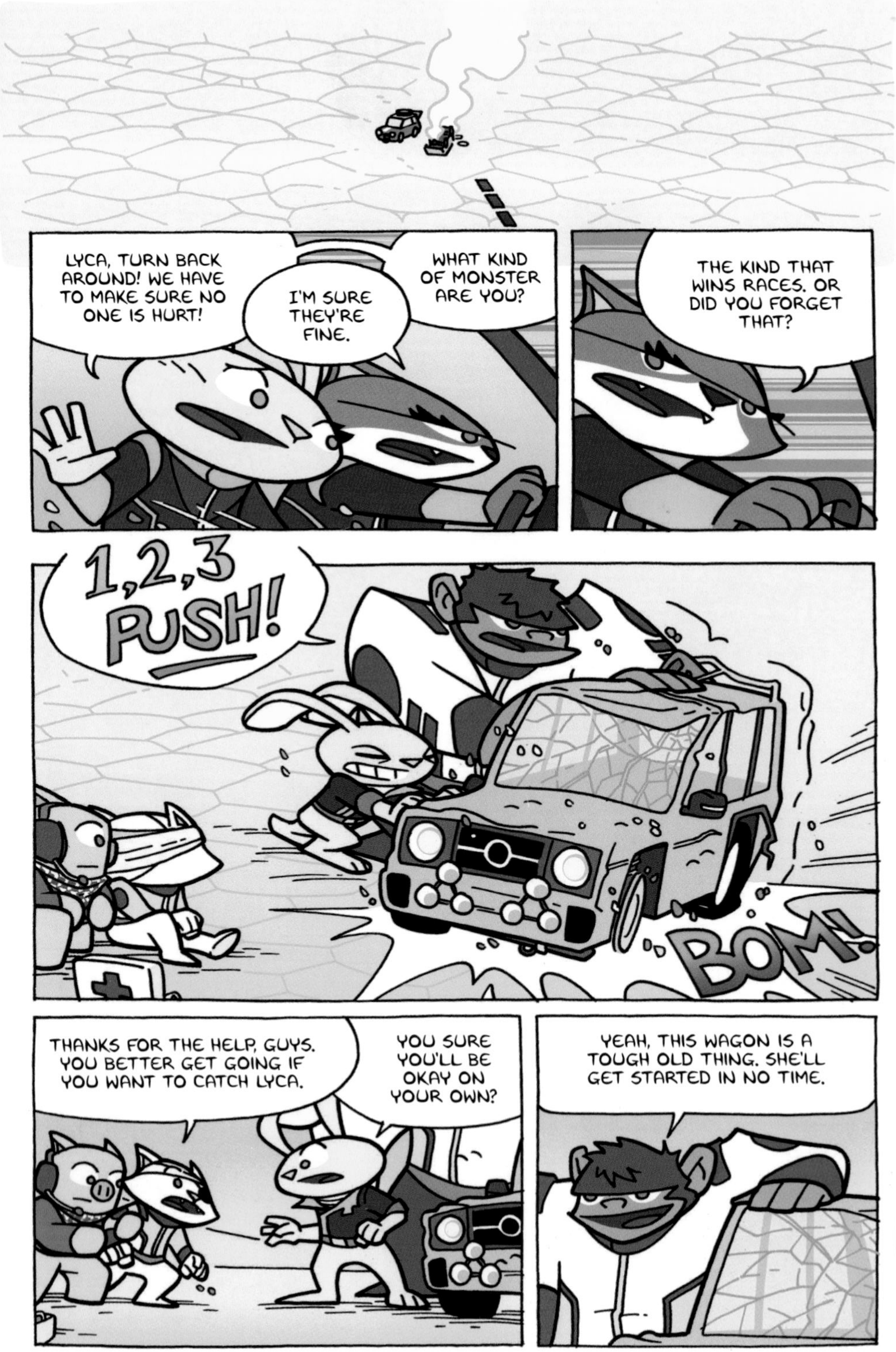
LYCA, TURN BACK AROUND! WE HAVE TO MAKE SURE NO ONE IS HURT!
I'M SURE THEY'RE FINE.
WHAT KIND OF MONSTER ARE YOU?
THE KIND THAT WINS RACES. OR DID YOU FORGET THAT?
1,2,3 PUSH!
BOM!
THANKS FOR THE HELP, GUYS. YOU BETTER GET GOING IF YOU WANT TO CATCH LYCA.
YOU SURE YOU'LL BE OKAY ON YOUR OWN?
YEAH, THIS WAGON IS A TOUGH OLD THING. SHE'LL GET STARTED IN NO TIME.

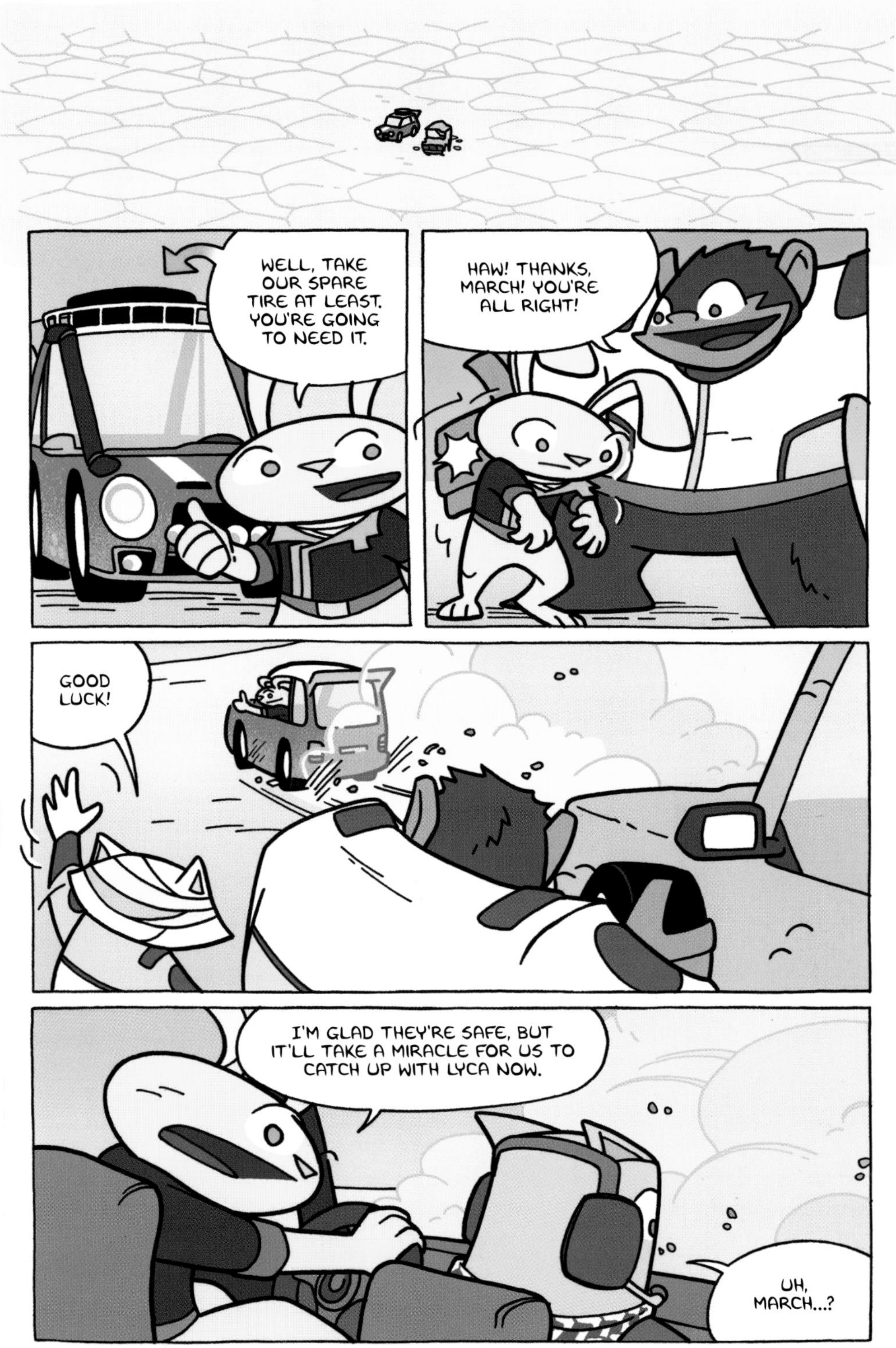
WELL, TAKE OUR SPARE TIRE AT LEAST. YOU'RE GOING TO NEED IT.
HAW! THANKS, MARCH! YOU'RE ALL RIGHT!
GOOD LUCK!
I'M GLAD THEY'RE SAFE, BUT IT'LL TAKE A MIRACLE FOR US TO CATCH UP WITH LYCA NOW.
UH, MARCH...?

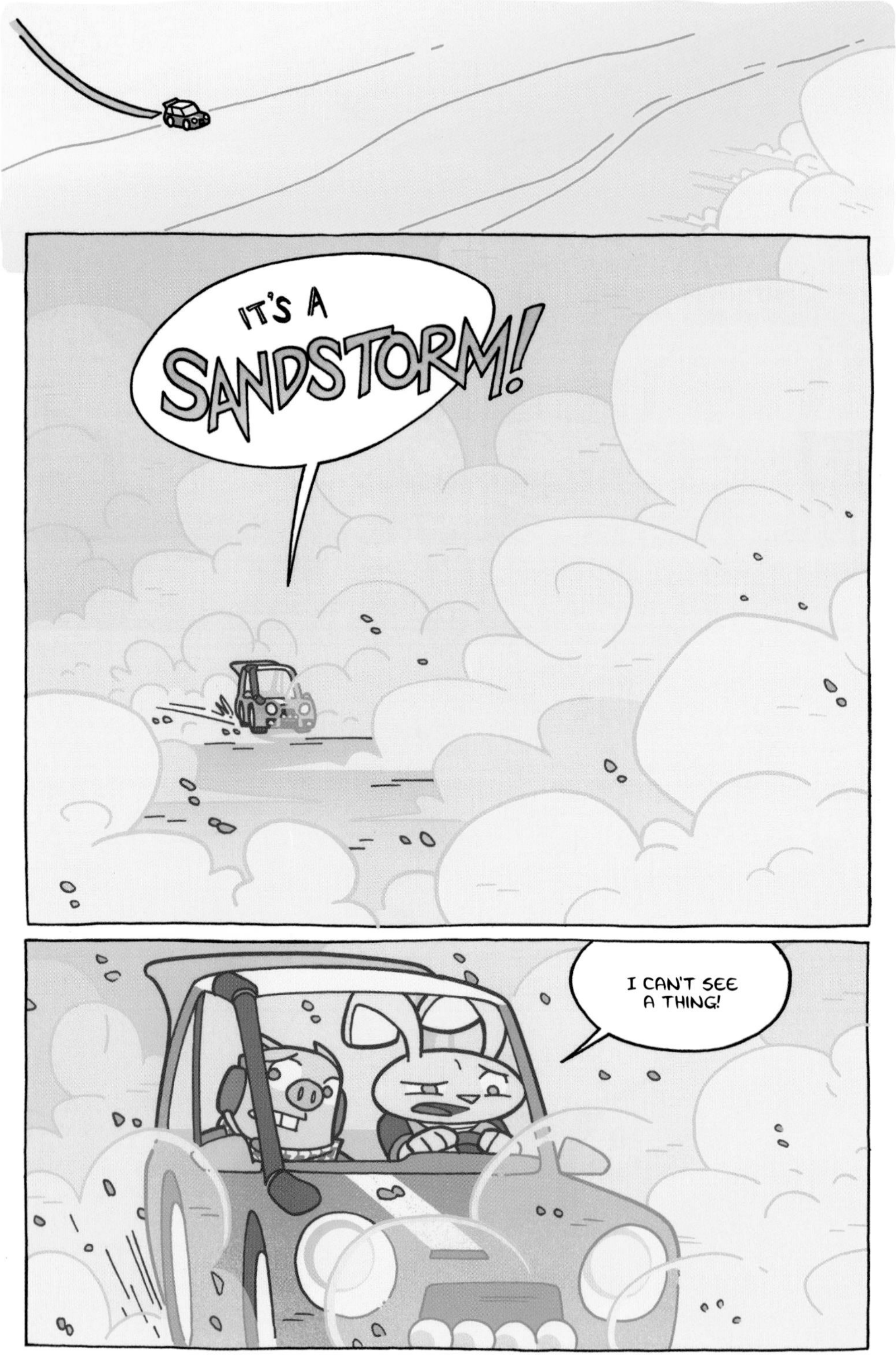
IT'S A SANDSTORM!
I CAN'T SEE A THING!

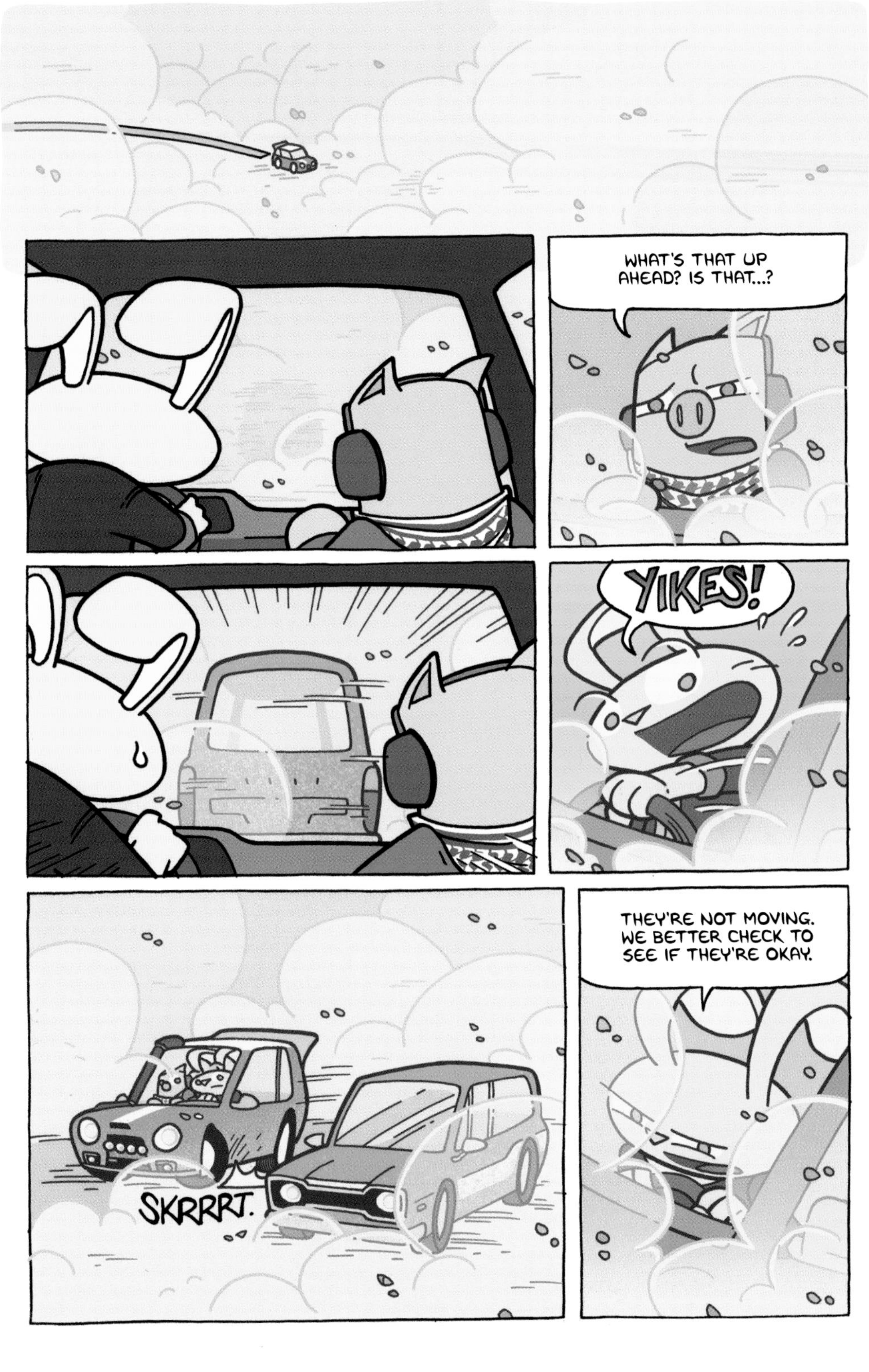
WHAT'S THAT UP AHEAD? IS THAT...?
YIKES!
SKRRRT.
THEY'RE NOT MOVING. WE BETTER CHECK TO SEE IF THEY'RE OKAY.

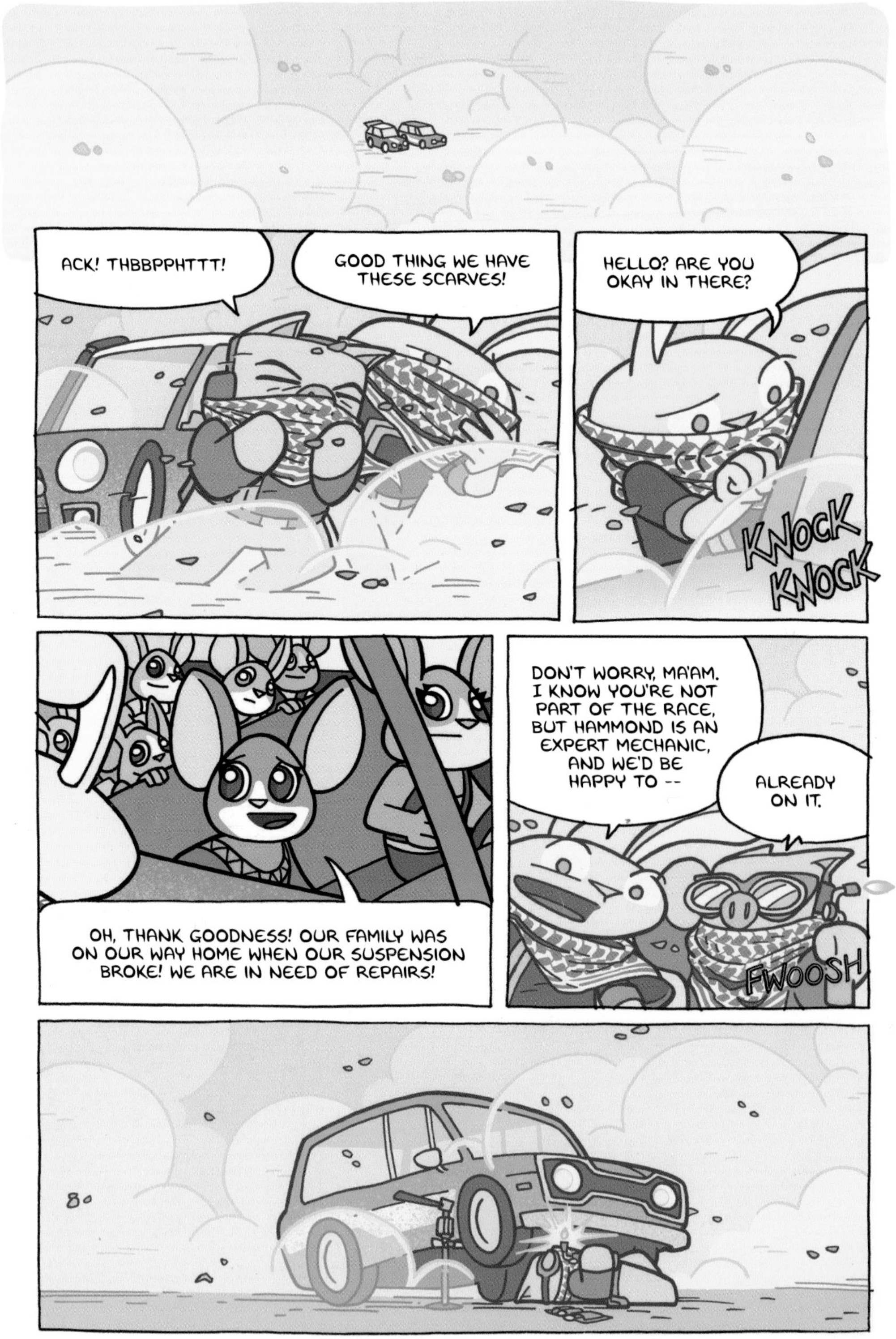
ACK! THBBPPHTTT!
GOOD THING WE HAVE THESE SCARVES!
HELLO? ARE YOU OKAY IN THERE?
KNOCK KNOCK
OH, THANK GOODNESS! OUR FAMILY WAS ON OUR WAY HOME WHEN OUR SUSPENSION BROKE! WE ARE IN NEED OF REPAIRS!
DON'T WORRY, MA'AM. I KNOW YOU'RE NOT PART OF THE RACE, BUT HAMMOND IS AN EXPERT MECHANIC, AND WE'D BE HAPPY TO --
ALREADY ON IT.
FWOOSH

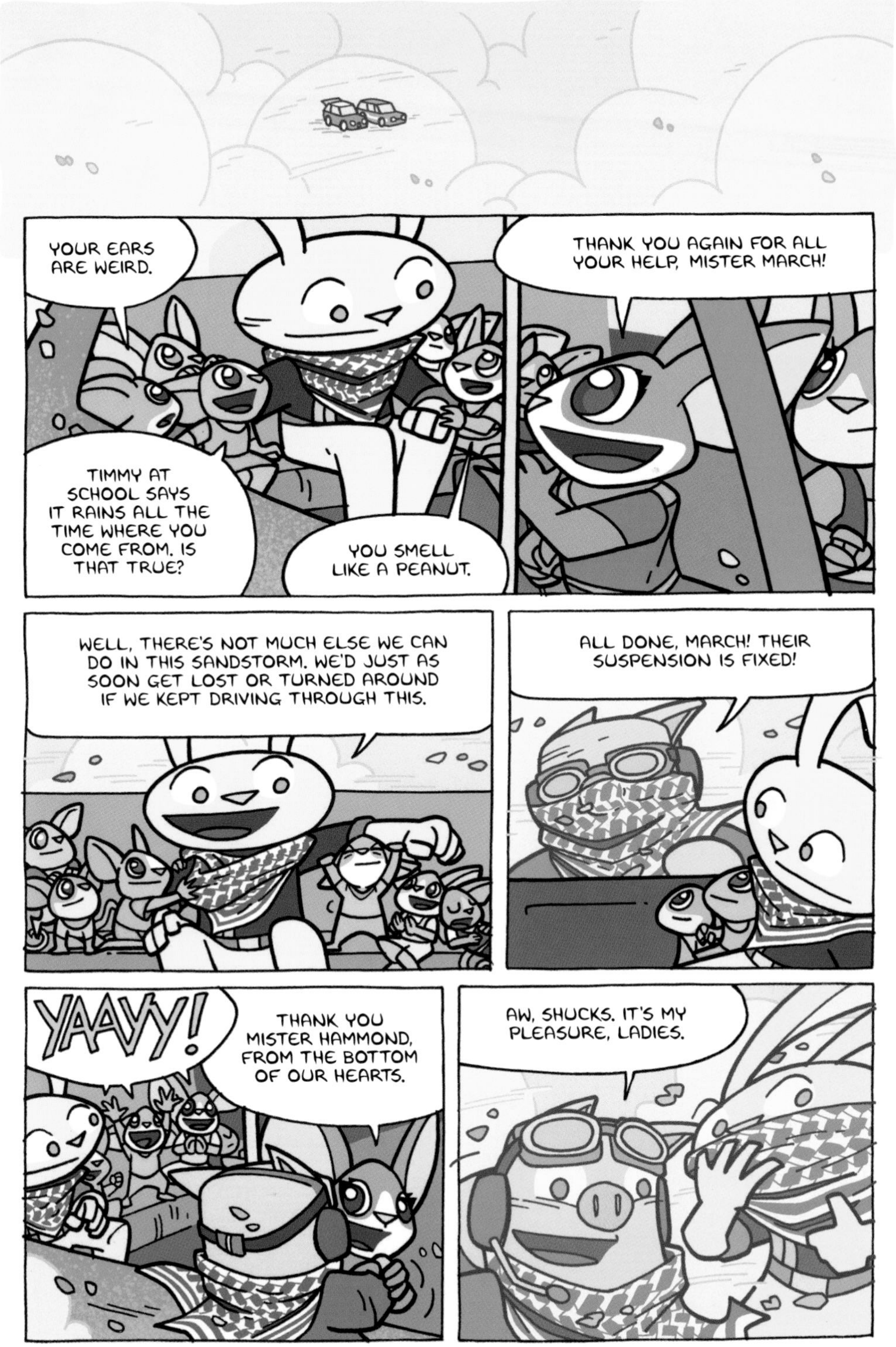
YOUR EARS ARE WEIRD.
TIMMY AT SCHOOL SAYS IT RAINS ALL THE TIME WHERE YOU COME FROM. IS THAT TRUE?
YOU SMELL LIKE A PEANUT.
THANK YOU AGAIN FOR ALL YOUR HELP, MISTER MARCH!
WELL, THERE'S NOT MUCH ELSE WE CAN DO IN THIS SANDSTORM. WE'D JUST AS SOON GET LOST OR TURNED AROUND IF WE KEPT DRIVING THROUGH THIS.
ALL DONE, MARCH! THEIR SUSPENSION IS FIXED!
YAAYY!
THANK YOU MISTER HAMMOND, FROM THE BOTTOM OF OUR HEARTS.
AW, SHUCKS. IT'S MY PLEASURE, LADIES.

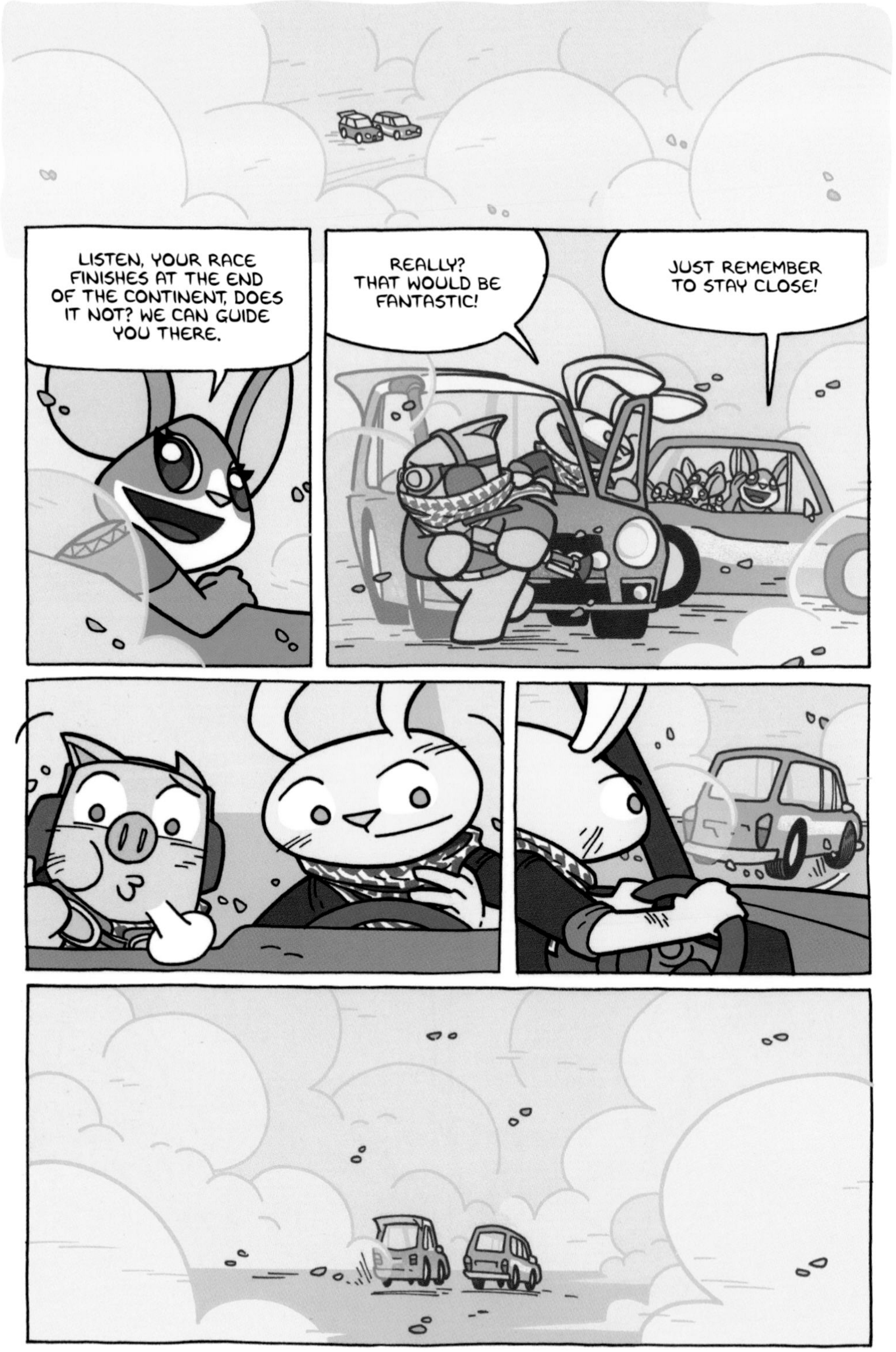
LISTEN, YOUR RACE FINISHES AT THE END OF THE CONTINENT, DOES IT NOT? WE CAN GUIDE YOU THERE.
REALLY? THAT WOULD BE FANTASTIC!
JUST REMEMBER TO STAY CLOSE!

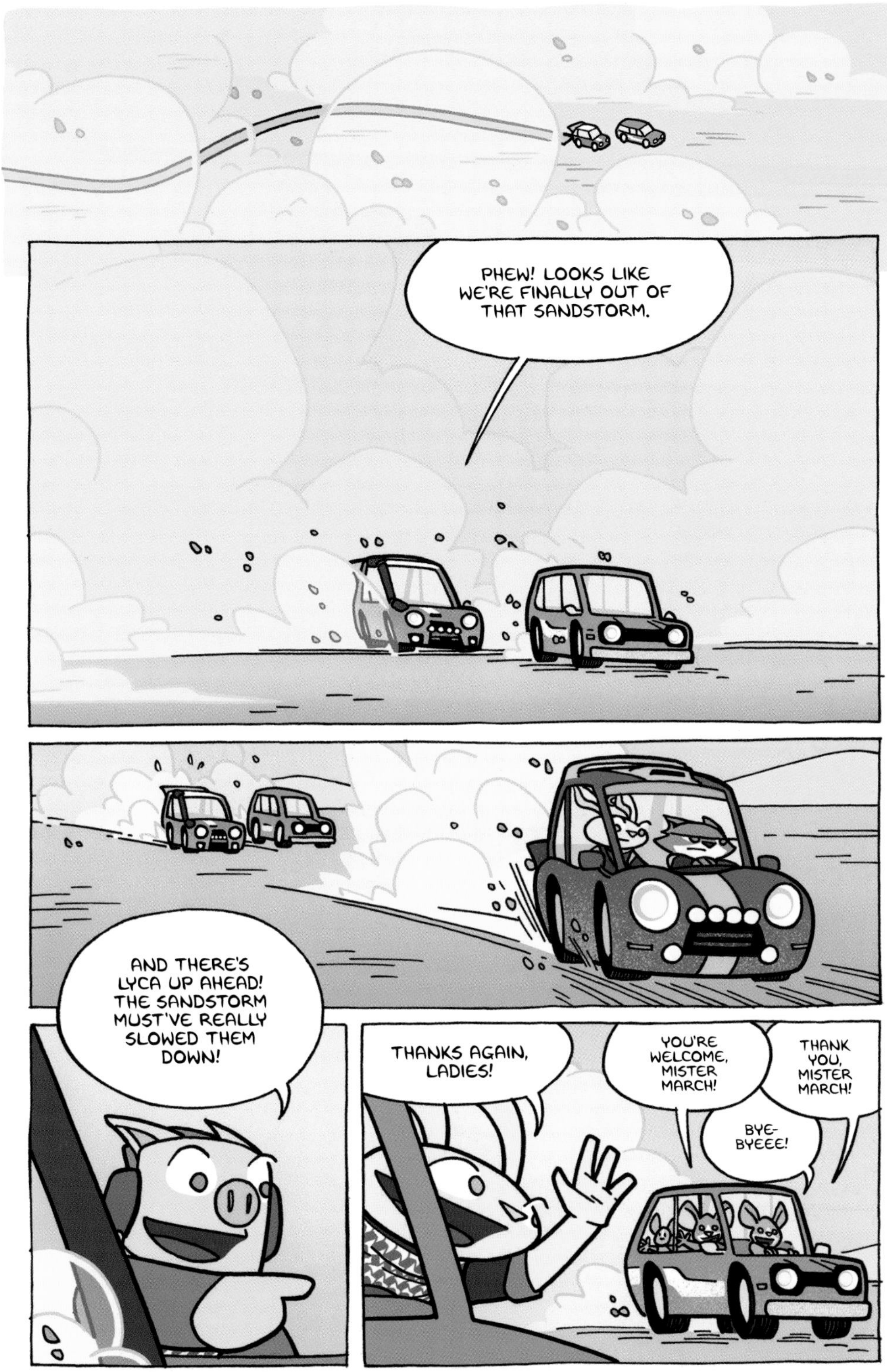
PHEW! LOOKS LIKE WE'RE FINALLY OUT OF THAT SANDSTORM.
AND THERE'S LYCA UP AHEAD! THE SANDSTORM MUST'VE REALLY SLOWED THEM DOWN!
THANKS AGAIN, LADIES!
YOU'RE WELCOME, MISTER MARCH!
THANK YOU, MISTER MARCH!
BYE-BYEEE!

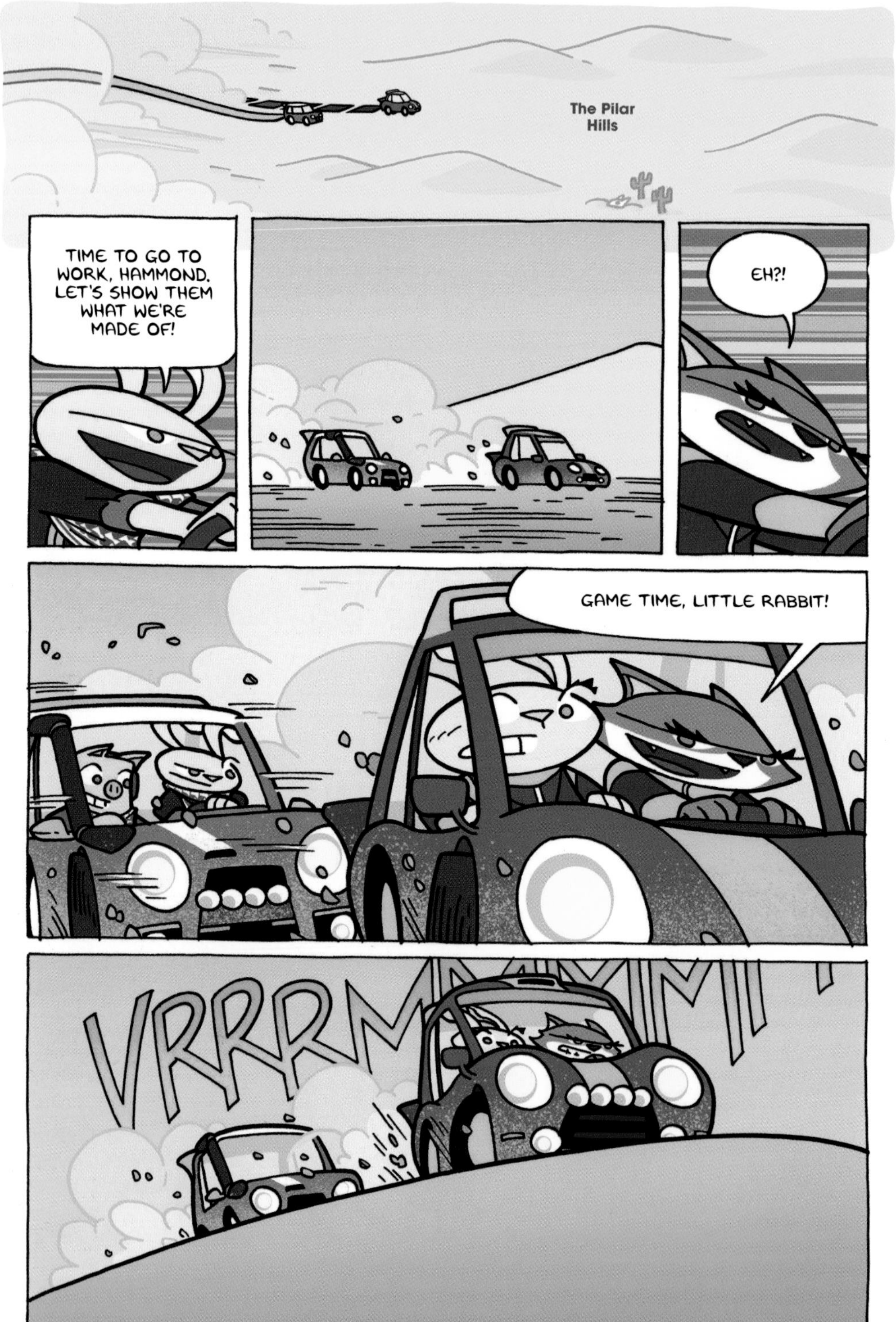

The Pilar Hills
TIME TO GO TO WORK, HAMMOND. LET'S SHOW THEM WHAT WE'RE MADE OF!
EH?!
GAME TIME, LITTLE RABBIT!
VRRRMMMM!!

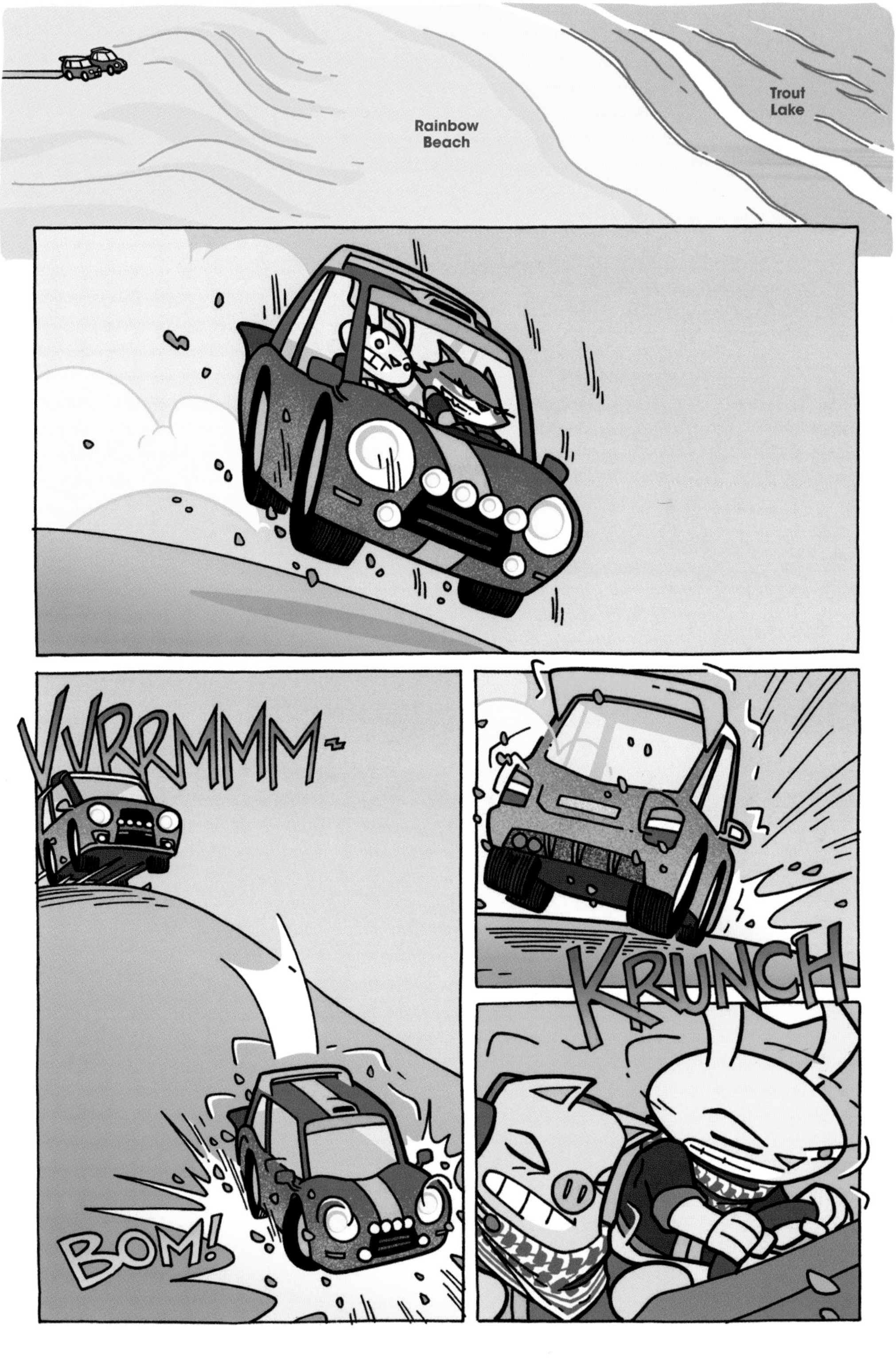
Rainbow Beach
Trout Lake
VVRRMMM
BOM!
KRUNCH

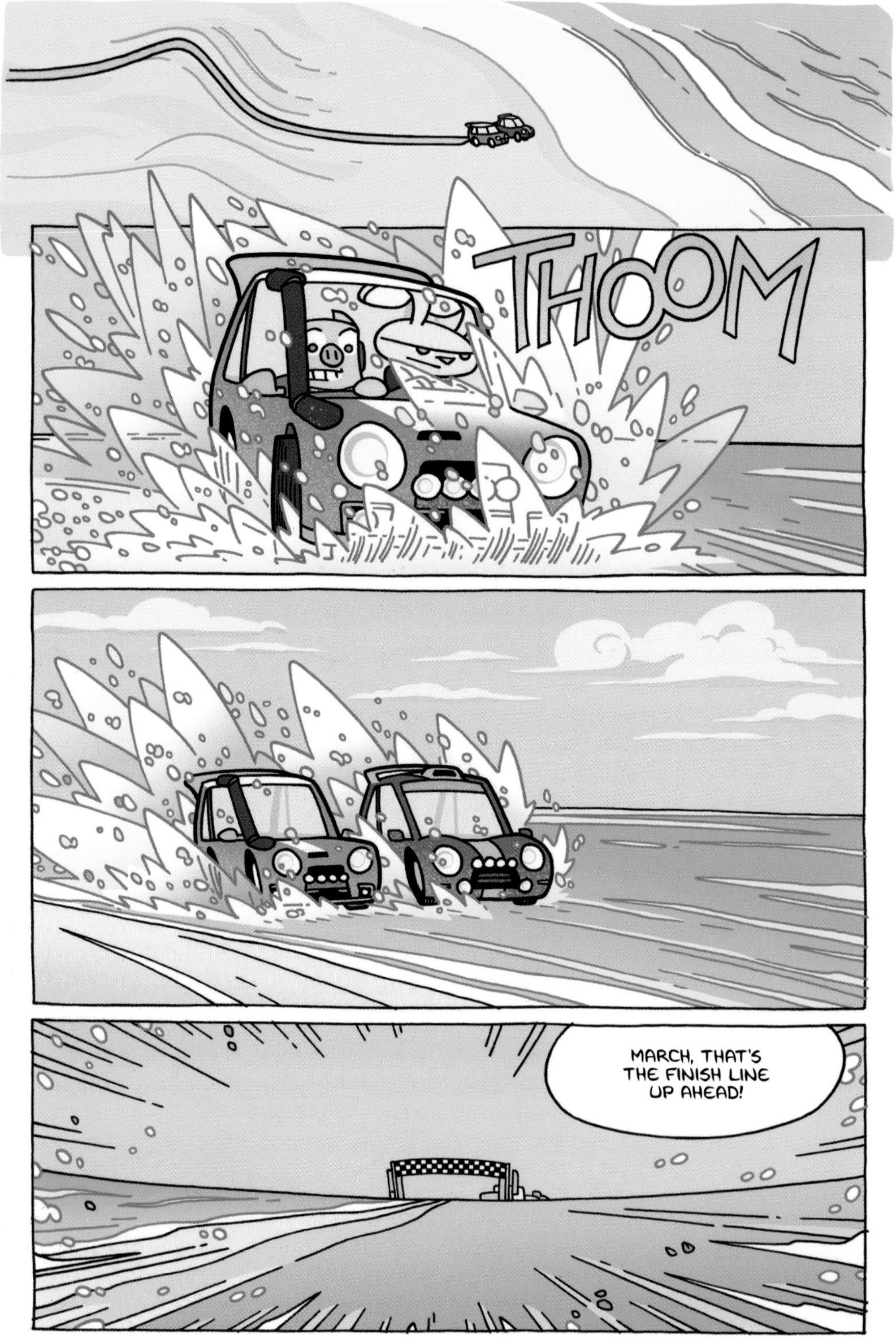
THOOM
MARCH, THAT'S THE FINISH LINE UP AHEAD!

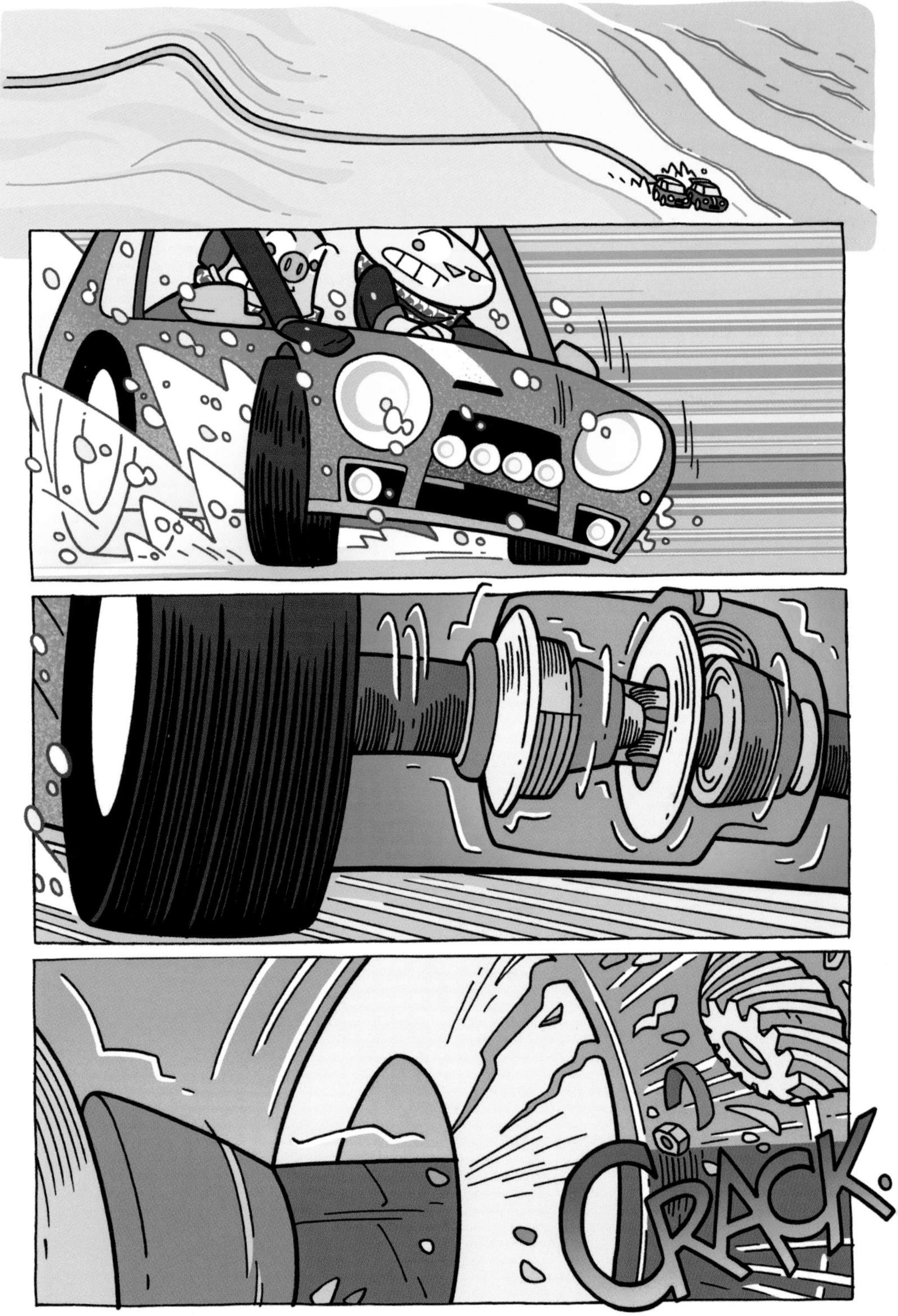
CRACK

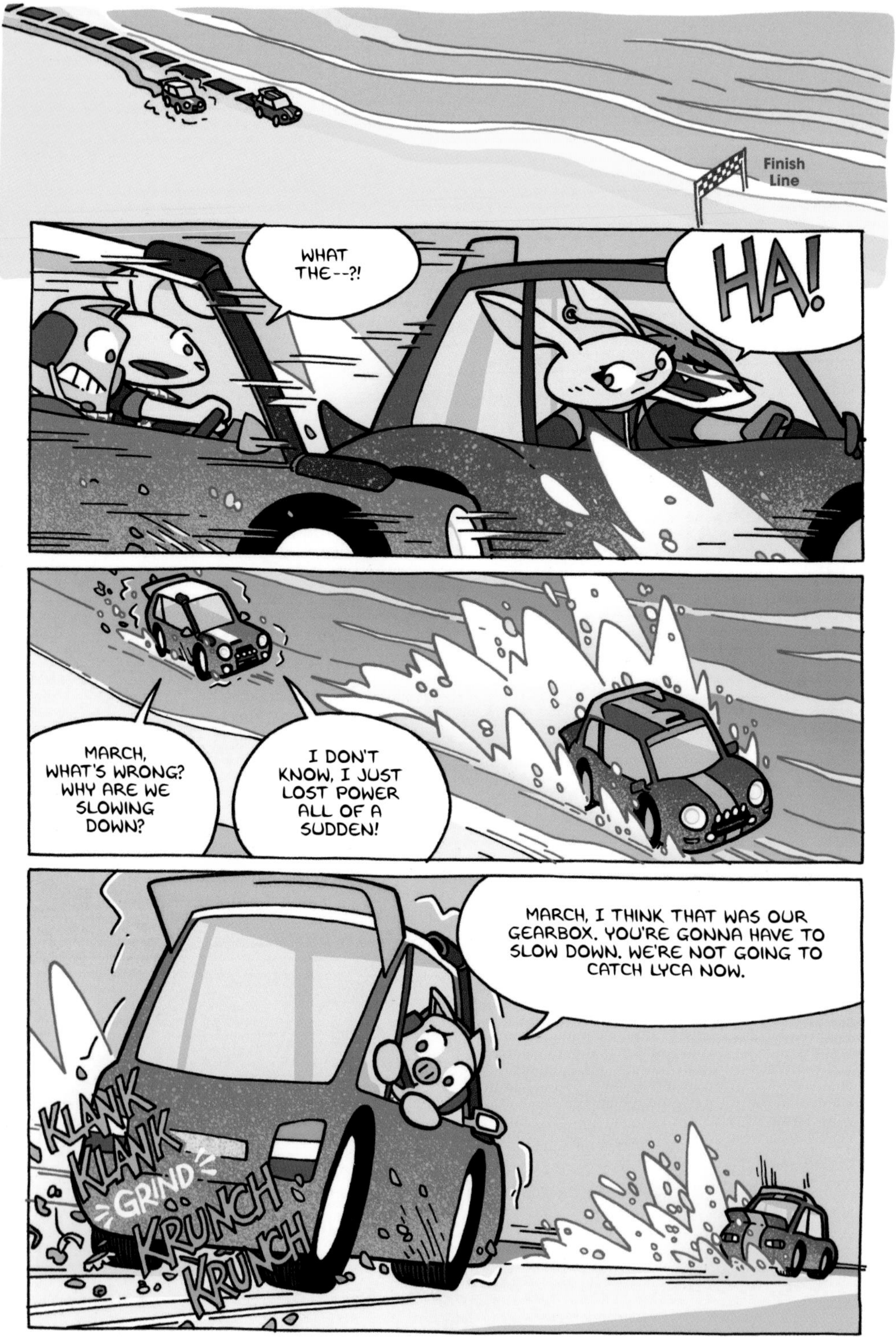
Finish Line
WHAT THE--?!
HA!
MARCH, WHAT'S WRONG? WHY ARE WE SLOWING DOWN?
I DON'T KNOW, I JUST LOST POWER ALL OF A SUDDEN!
MARCH, I THINK THAT WAS OUR GEARBOX. YOU'RE GONNA HAVE TO SLOW DOWN. WE'RE NOT GOING TO CATCH LYCA NOW.
KLANK KLANK GRIND KRUNCH KRUNCH

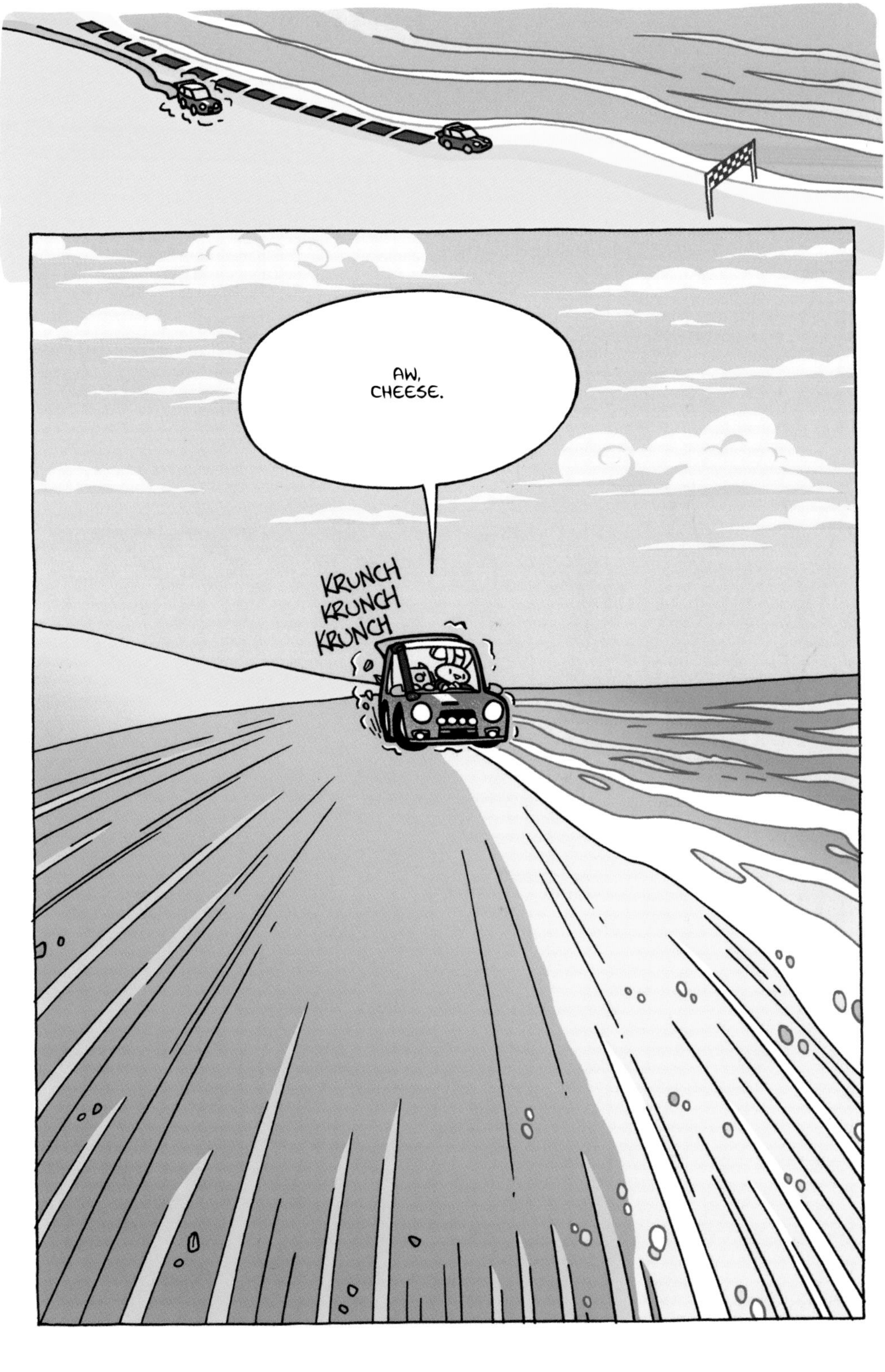
AW, CHEESE.
KRUNCH
KRUNCH
KRUNCH

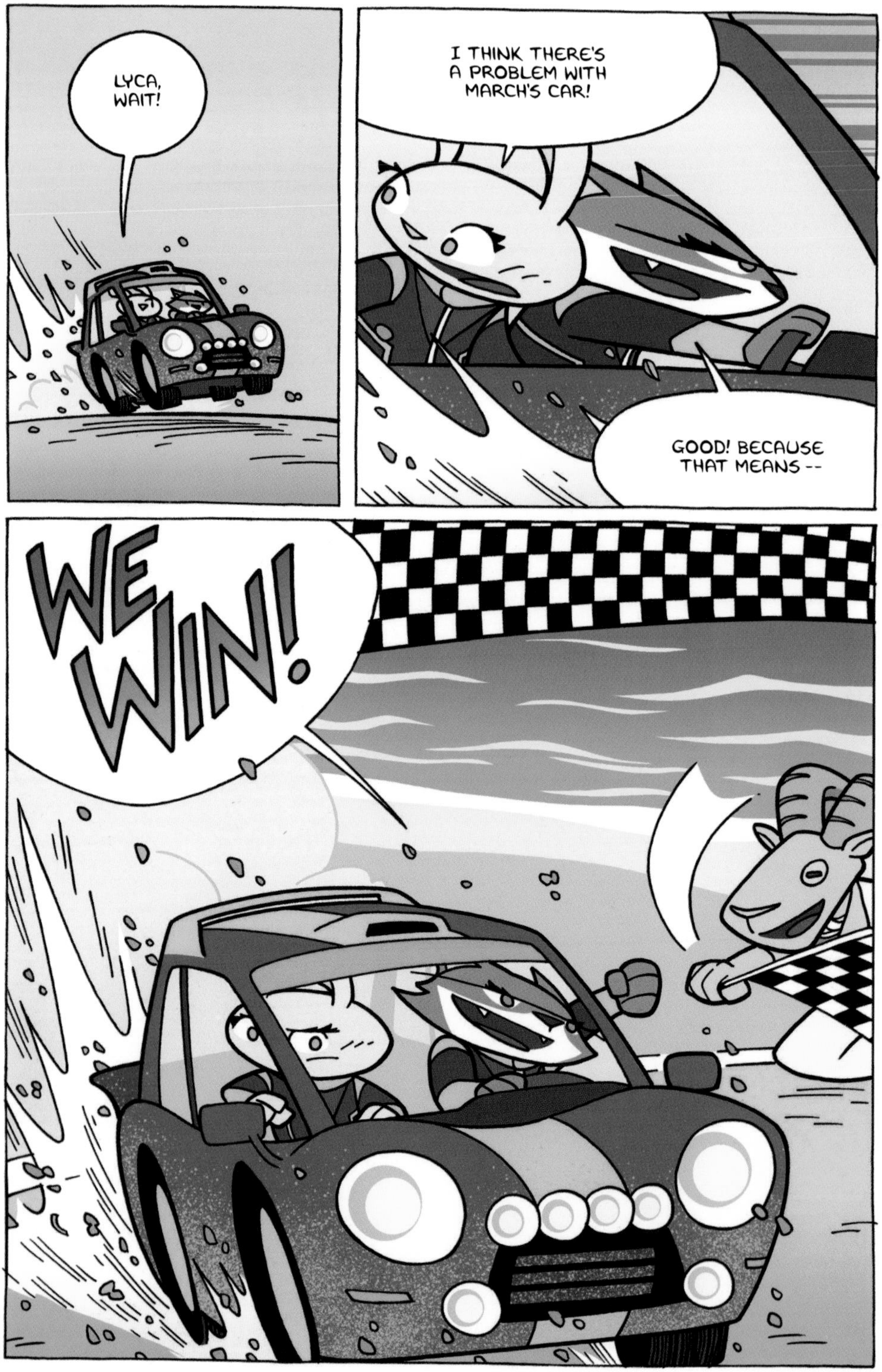
LYCA, WAIT!
I THINK THERE'S A PROBLEM WITH MARCH'S CAR!
GOOD! BECAUSE THAT MEANS --
WE WIN!

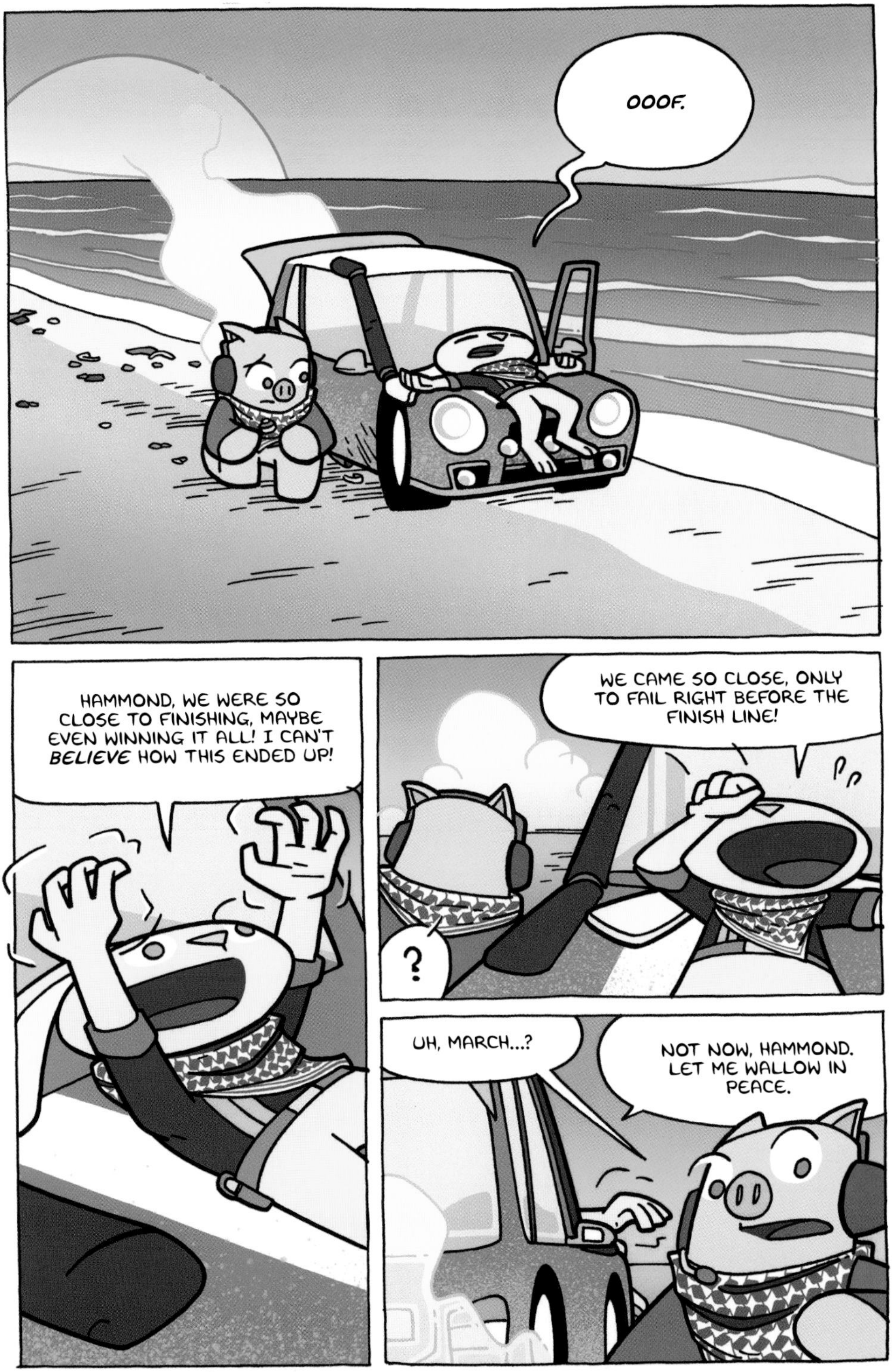
OOOF.
HAMMOND, WE WERE SO CLOSE TO FINISHING, MAYBE EVEN WINNING IT ALL! I CAN'T *BELIEVE* HOW THIS ENDED UP!
WE CAME SO CLOSE, ONLY TO FAIL RIGHT BEFORE THE FINISH LINE!
?
UH, MARCH...?
NOT NOW, HAMMOND. LET ME WALLOW IN PEACE.

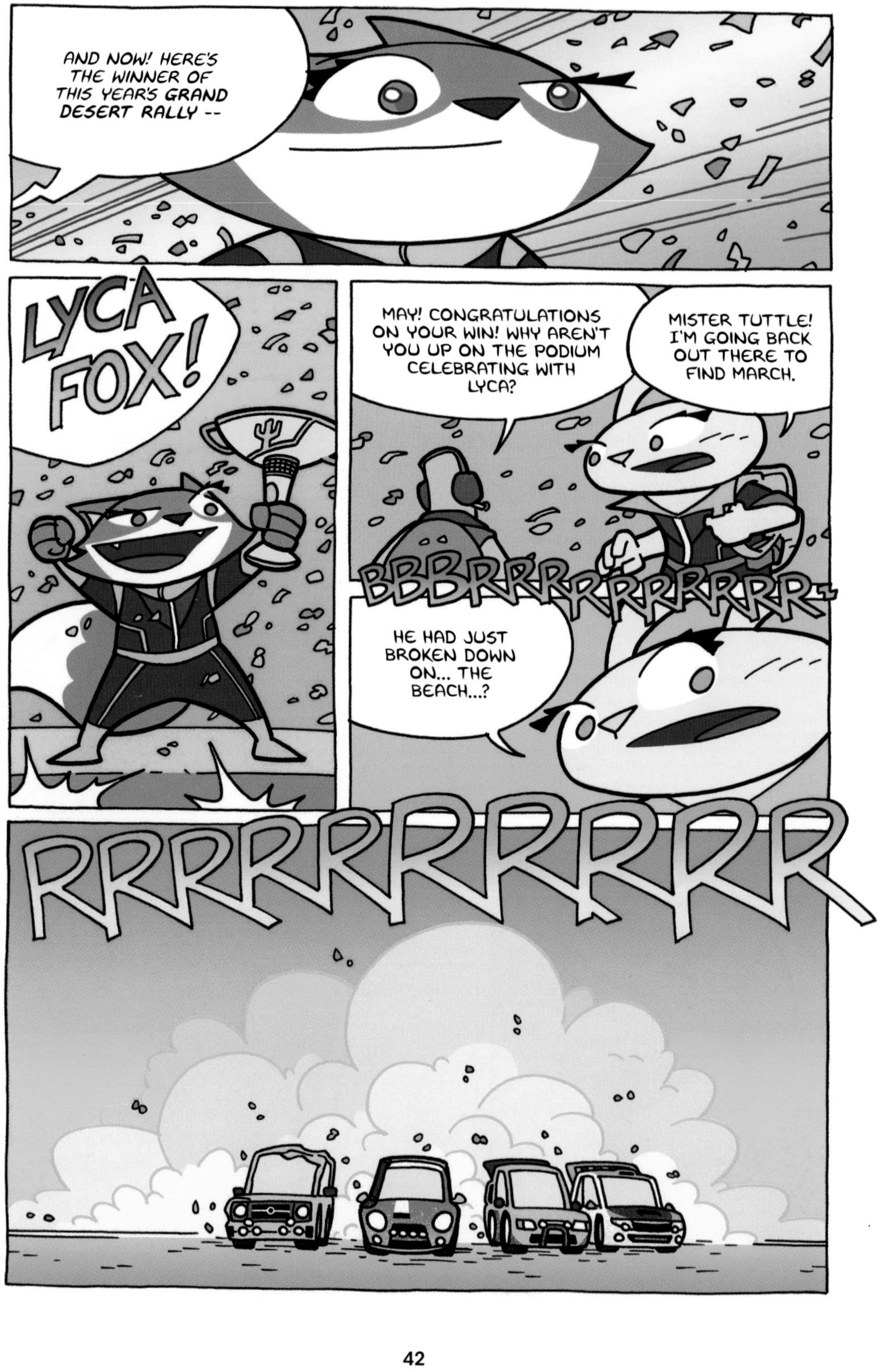
AND NOW! HERE'S THE WINNER OF THIS YEAR'S GRAND DESERT RALLY --
LYCA FOX!
MAY! CONGRATULATIONS ON YOUR WIN! WHY AREN'T YOU UP ON THE PODIUM CELEBRATING WITH LYCA?
MISTER TUTTLE! I'M GOING BACK OUT THERE TO FIND MARCH.
BBBRRRRRRRRRRRR
HE HAD JUST BROKEN DOWN ON... THE BEACH...?
RRRRRRRRRRR

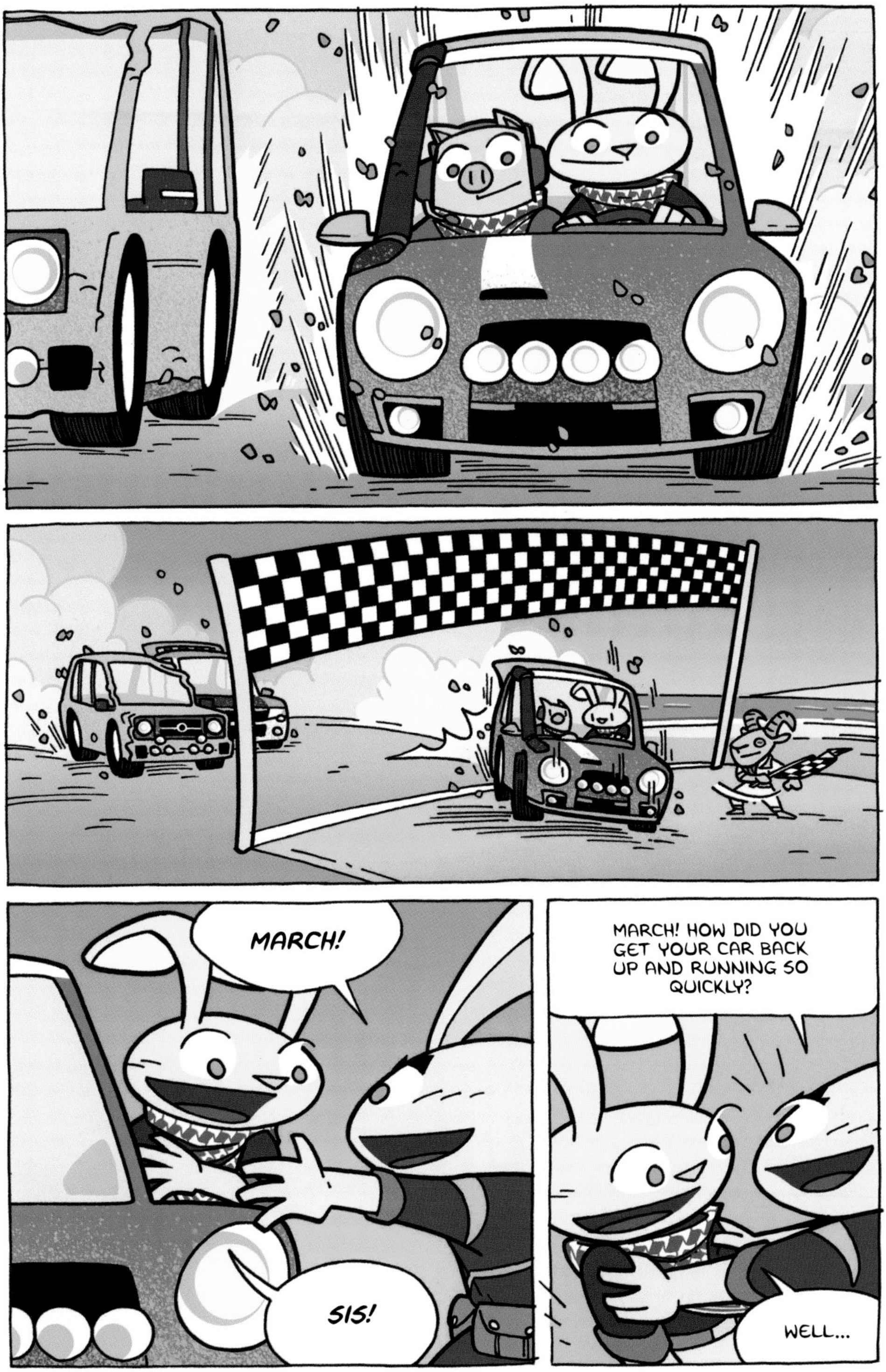
MARCH!
SIS!
MARCH! HOW DID YOU GET YOUR CAR BACK UP AND RUNNING SO QUICKLY?
WELL...

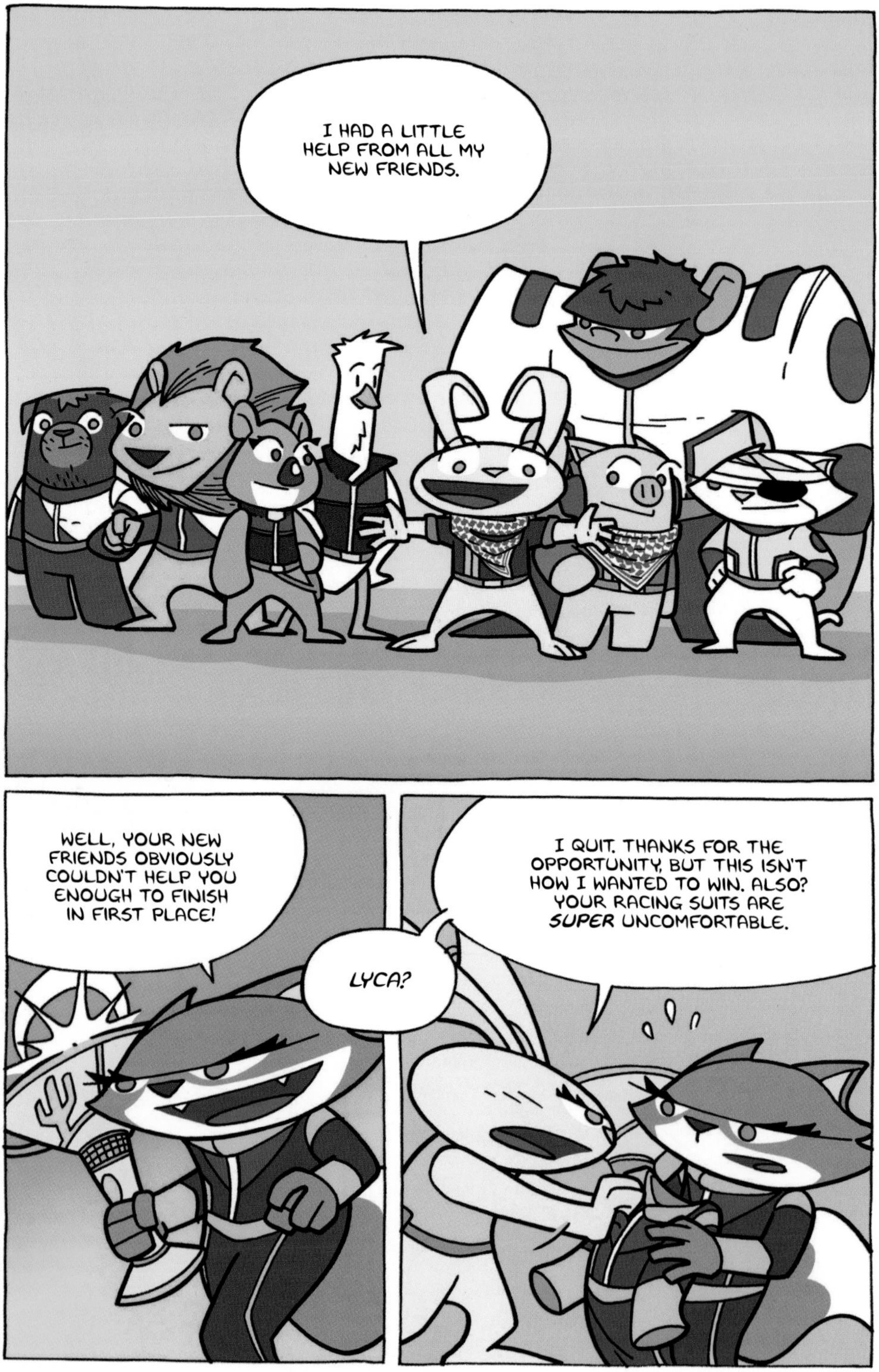
I HAD A LITTLE HELP FROM ALL MY NEW FRIENDS.
WELL, YOUR NEW FRIENDS OBVIOUSLY COULDN'T HELP YOU ENOUGH TO FINISH IN FIRST PLACE!
LYCA?
I QUIT. THANKS FOR THE OPPORTUNITY, BUT THIS ISN'T HOW I WANTED TO WIN. ALSO? YOUR RACING SUITS ARE SUPER UNCOMFORTABLE.

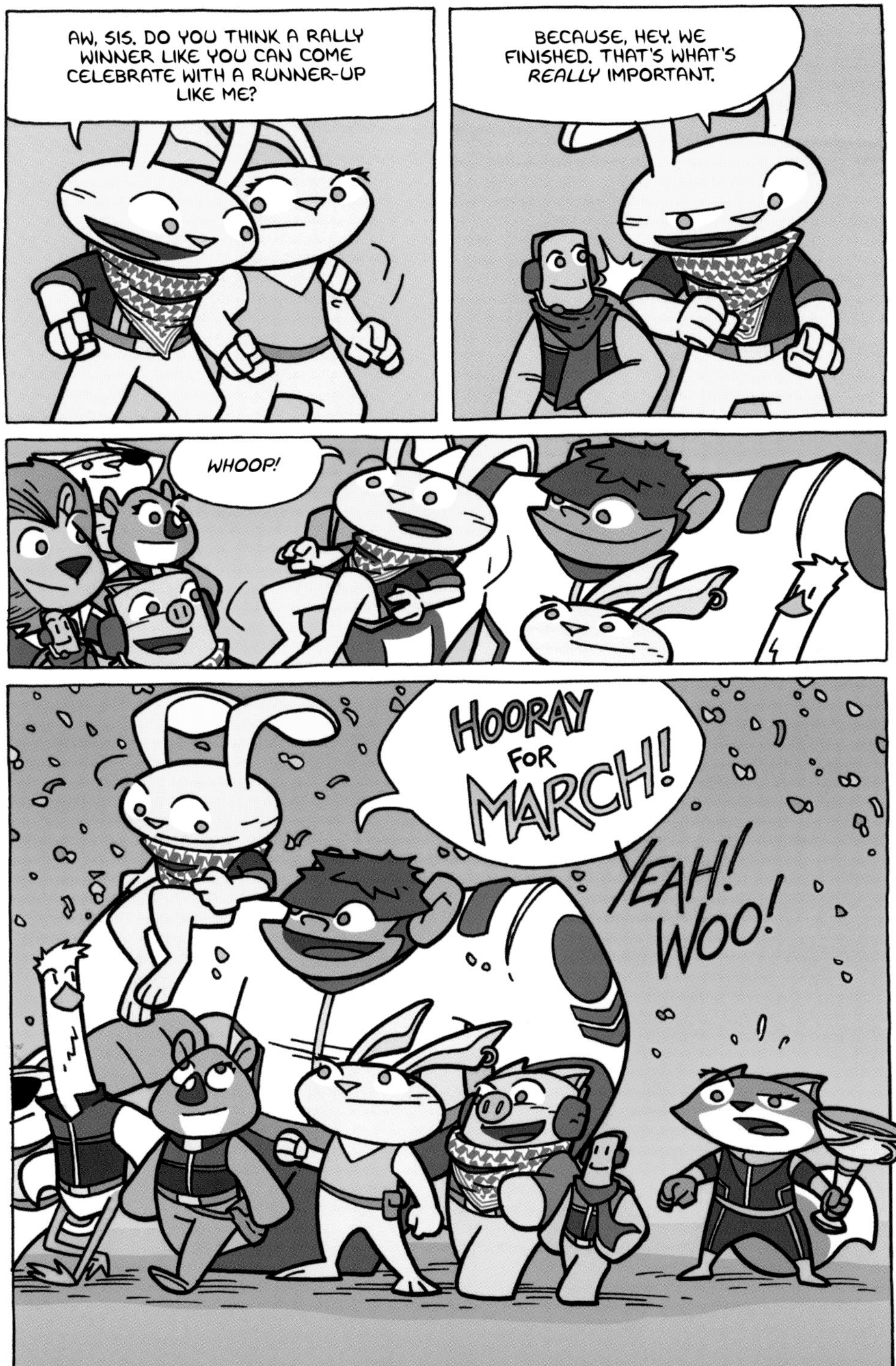
AW, SIS. DO YOU THINK A RALLY WINNER LIKE YOU CAN COME CELEBRATE WITH A RUNNER-UP LIKE ME?
BECAUSE, HEY. WE FINISHED. THAT'S WHAT'S *REALLY* IMPORTANT.
WHOOP!
HOORAY FOR MARCH!
YEAH! WOO!

SKETCHES

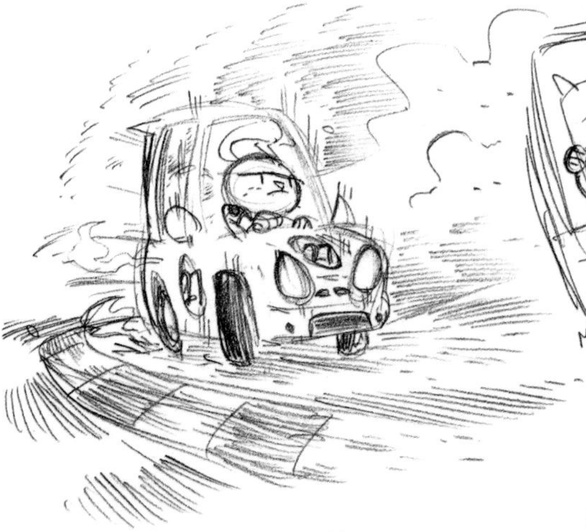

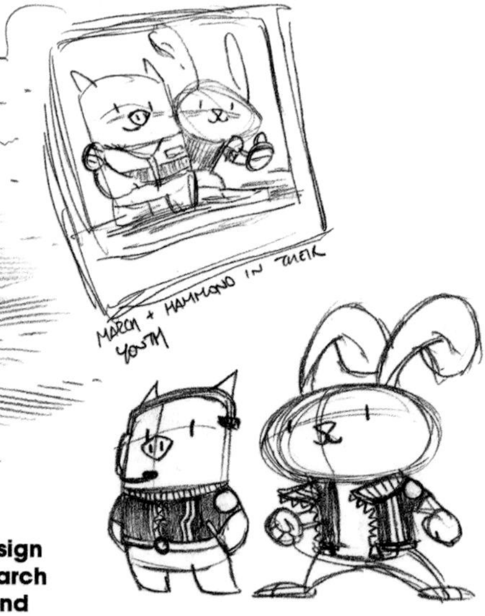
MARCH + HAMMOND IN THEIR YOUTH

Very early design sketches of March and Hammond

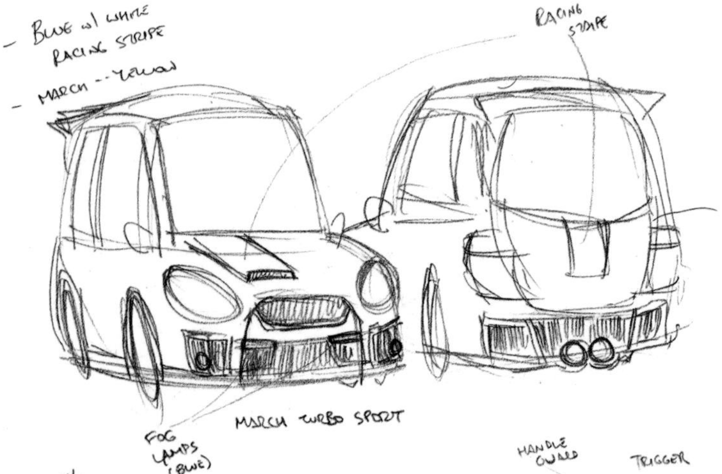
- BLUE w/ WHITE RACING STRIPE
- MARCH -- YELLOW
RACING STRIPE
MARCH TURBO SPORT
FOG LAMPS (BLUE)

Early design sketches of March and Lyca's cars

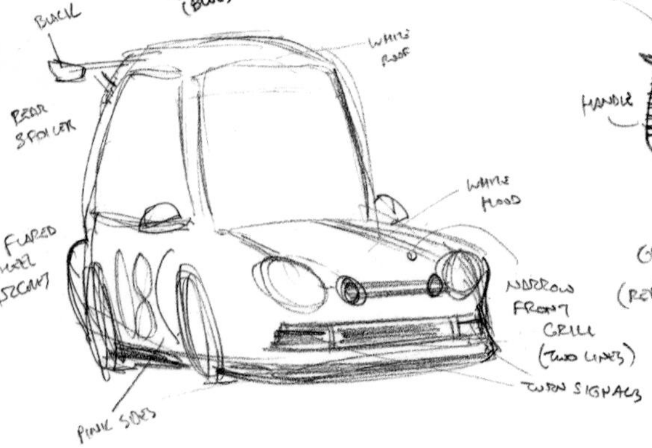
BLACK
WHITE ROOF
REAR SPOILER
WHITE HOOD
FLARED WHEEL ARCHES
NARROW FRONT GRILL (TWO LINES)
TURN SIGNALS
PINK SIDES

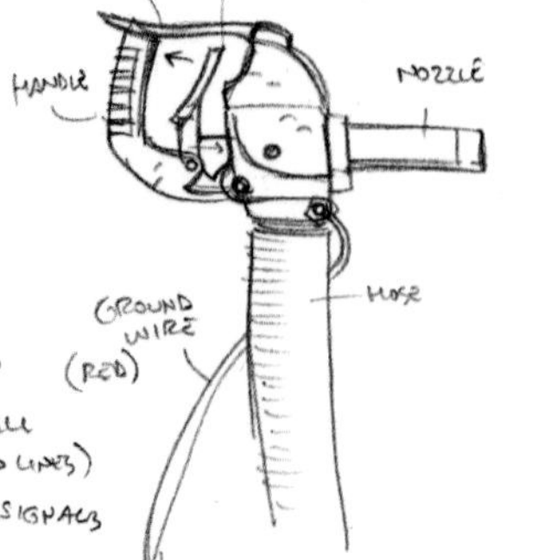
HANDLE GUARD
TRIGGER
FUEL PUMP
HANDLE
NOZZLE
HOSE
GROUND WIRE (RED)

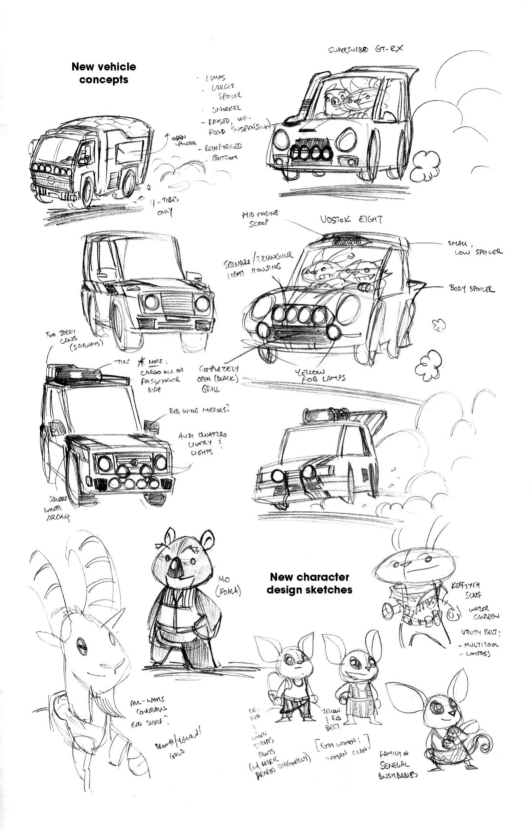

New vehicle concepts

New character design sketches

KEAN SOO

Kean Soo was born in the United Kingdom, grew up in various parts of Canada and Hong Kong, trained as an electrical engineer, and now draws comics for a living. A former assistant editor and contributor for the FLIGHT comics anthology, Kean also created the award-winning Jellaby series of graphic novels.

Kean's first date with his wife was a month-long drive across Italy and the South of France in a Fiat 500.

Kean would also like to thank Judy Hansen, Donnie Lemke, Brann Garvey, Tony Cliff, Kazu Kibuishi, everyone in the FLIGHT crew, and Tory Woollcott for making March Grand Prix such a joy to work on.